Alfonso A Matos (Author)

"Method vs Results- the world's never ending quest or determination to rise to the top. In spite of their differences, both can work in harmony but their results stands alone. Forget about the "how" and remove your fears, just focus on getting it done and act." A.A. Matos

Thank you God for all your blessings to my family and me, for the strength, you give me each day, and for all the people around me who make life more meaningful.

CHAPTER 1

"Where do you think you're going?" Emily's boss asks with rapt concern.

Emily sighs as she turns around to face her irritated boss. As always, his eyes bulge out with emotions akin to anger, but Emily could care less. All-day, she's been on her feet, and she certainly could use a break. Her shoulders groan loudly with every movement she makes, and her stomach isn't helping matters, hitting her with deep pangs every few seconds. It's time to go home, her body had screamed, and she listened to it. After all, the closing time is five p.m.

"Home. I'm going home," She stares at him, unblinking. Ivan stares back, quiet. His silence is a threat that Emily recognizes.

"There are still customers waiting to be served. You know we are short on staff," He deadpans. Emily wraps the scarf in her hand around her neck with a blank expression on her face despite the growing fear within her. Her fingers are growing sweaty, but she ignores it.

"There's a lengthy list of applicants. You need to stop being picky and choose some waiters." Ivan makes a sound in his throat, "I told you I'm trying to select the best of the best, Emily. Just be a little more patient with me for goodness's sake!"

"It's been two months, Ivan, and as patient as I'd love to be, I'm not willing to pay with my free time and energy tonight. You've worn me out. Have a good night, Ivan."

Before Ivan can say another word, Emily steps out of the stuffy kitchen. The cool evening breeze hits her face softly as she walks towards her old beat-up Chevy. The sun is setting in the sky, casting an orange hue across town. This is Emily's best part of the day, but Ivan has had her working late for so many nights that she barely remembered what a setting sky looked like. As much as she hated it, she didn't have a choice either. There's truly little you can do with a high school diploma. Things had already been beyond terrible several months earlier before Ivan, Before Tom...

The familiar blue color of her Chevy instantly soothes her and the minute she's settled behind the wheel, she feels the tension ease slightly out of her body. Exhaling loudly, Emily glances at the passenger's seat. Her daughter's Barbie doll is on the seat, one arm missing. With a nostalgic sigh, Emily sets out and begins to head home. On the radio, a country song is playing but Emily is barely paying attention, her mind is far away. Emily thinks to herself as she controls the wheel with one arm; first I'll grab a glass of wine, then, a bubble bath, afterward, probably a box of pizza or some macaroni and cheese. The distant thought of her children pops back into her mind, especially Emil. He has been acting rather strange for a while now...Emily sighs as she lets the thought filter out of her mind. Emil has always been a strange kid, nothing new there.

The artist singing on the radio sounds like an old friend of Emily's, someone she used to know. That's how she often remembers things - in sounds, in bits and pieces. She makes a mental note to remind her daughter to practice for her upcoming recital.

"Home! Home!" Emily states as she arrives home, exhaling loudly, Emily opens the door to her house and pulls the keys out of the lock. The living room is dark, devoid of any presence. Emily sets her keys on an adjacent table, walks to the kitchen, and turns on a kitchen light. Emily glances at the kitchen sink and is surprised to find it empty. Did Tom and the kids eat out again? she wonders as she walks inches close to the fridge. Since Tom came into their lives, he's been big on indulging the kids, claiming they deserve it. Judging from the quiet house, Emily knows the kids are asleep and the thought excites her even more. A bottle of wine stares back at her as she grabs it. A quiet house, wine, and a long bath. It's the perfect night.

The wine tastes divine against Emily's thirsty lips. She savors it before swallowing and sighing in relief. As she pours another glass, she feels a gaze on her. Emily looks to her left and finds her older son, Emil, crouched in the corner, near one of the kitchen chairs. Startled, she places the glass carefully on the kitchen table. Emil stares back at his mother, quiet. Emily is about to ask him a question when she notices that he is naked. Is this some kind of game? Emil is naked and wet with oil. Emily can see blood under Emil's buttocks.

"Emil, what did you do?" Emily asks with a hand on her hip. When her son does not respond, Emily inches closer and realizes tears dripping out Emil's eyes.

"Why are you here naked? Why are you crying?" Emily scoots down, surveying her son carefully. Her heart pulses rapidly within her chest as her son sniffs, his eyes swollen.

"Tom hurt me, mom. He did something bad to me." Emil's words nearly cause the oxygen in Emily's lungs to evaporate. It takes Emily a few seconds to regain her composure. Nothing is wrong, Emily, breathe, she says to herself.

"Tom loves you, baby. He would never hurt you," Emily says in a shaky voice as she reaches for Emil's hands. His hands feel cold in hers and Emily nearly pulls away in shock.

Emily finds herself saying in a cold voice, "Emil, think carefully about what you are saying," Her son only appears even more hurt as he shakes his head vigorously.

"He touched my private parts and hurt me in the back," he whispers. A cold dark feeling spreads through Emily's chest and she finds herself breathing loudly as she stares at Emil. The peace and sanity she had managed to build for her kids is now a glass house and Emily can feel the splinters going through the glass already.

"What? Did he do this to you?" Before Emil can respond, she launches further. "Are you making this up to get even with Tom for not allowing you to go to the park yesterday?", Emil closes his eyes, and more tears roll down, but Emily is too engulfed to see him. Waves of anger and irritation rolls off her as she stares at her son.

"Emil, your father left me years ago and doesn't even have the balls to send money or help us in any shape or form, Tom gives everything to us, our lives have changed since I met him!"

Emil cries harder and Emily finds herself confused as she stares at her son. She is about to speak again when they hear a loud knock on the door. Glancing at Emil, she gestures for him to stay on the ground as she rises. She can feel the weariness in her bones as she moves in the dark living room. When she pulls the door open, she finds a great shock, standing outside armed to their teeth are police officers who do not look happy.

Her perfect night has been ruined and everything around her goes foggy.

Memories from Emily's childhood assault her mind. Memories of the police running around their dingy neighborhood, chasing the boys who used to do drugs, occasionally firing at them. A post-traumatic image of the police arresting her father pops back into her mind and a strange coldness grips Emily's chest. Is she back in her childhood nightmare?

There are three officers on the porch. One is a female with brown hair and Emily can feel the sting of the officer's eyes. Swallowing her slobber, she then notices the man beside the female officer. His hand is on his waist, merely inches away from his gun. His dark eyes are trained on something behind her. The third officer standing in front of Emily has pale blue eyes and he looms over her, appearing intimidating. His lips are moving but Emily can barely hear a word. She blinks, hearing nothing. The police officer blinks and then repeats his words.

"Ma'am, we received a call from a child who stated that he was assaulted by his stepfather," The officer says loudly. The gravity of his words causes Emily to wince. Assault! Stepfather! Emily's stomach tightens.

"You have the wrong address, officer. No one here called the police." The words escape her mouth instantly. Emily is surprised at how calm she sounds. Her words however are not convincing enough for the police officer. He grabs his radio and speaks into it authoritatively.

"Dispatch, address check."

Emily's blood runs cold as the officers wait quietly to confirm the address. The voice in her head is yelling at her. Move, Emily! Close the door before they can say anything else! but Emily still is rooted in the same spot and when the dispatch speaks up, she's filled with dread.

7

"91, Cummingstone Street." The officer turns to her, a stern looks on his face as he nods at Emily.

"We have the right address. So, how many people live in this house?"

Emily takes a step back, realizing what this means. The glasshouse is rattling and letting the officers in would bring everything crashing down. Run, Emily! Lock the doors now!

"I have nothing to say to you, Officer. Am I under arrest?"

The officer looks incredulous. "No, why would you be under arrest?" Emily nods, satisfied as she takes another step backward, ready to shut the door in their faces. The second male officer with the dark eyes suddenly steps forward, his intense gaze on Emily. He looks like he's about to say something, but his attention is diverted. Emily follows the direction of his gaze and realizes what piqued his interest. Emil's blood has stained her hands and they can all clearly see it. Her heart jumps into her chest, mixing with the words that are trying to form in her defense. The officers however dash past her into the house.

"It's the Police! Emil, are you here? Talk to me, son," the officer with the dark ayes calls out into the dark living room. Emily enters quietly behind them, not making a sound. Her veins however pulse with fear and worries. The officers wait for Emil who is now moving towards them, a wet cloth covering his frontals. There's a sharp intake of breath within the room as the officer's watch Emil hobble.

Tears begin to build behind Emily's eyes as she watches her only son.

"Yes. I'm here." Emil says.

The officer crouches down and immediately pulls his radio out, his eyes still on Emil.

"Secure the woman and send the ambulance. I have a child victim of a possible criminal assault. Send a Sergeant and a Detective to our location," He barks into the radio as he reaches for Emil's bloody hands. When he receives response, the officer smiles softly at Emil as he pulls out a handkerchief to clean his face.

"Son, what happened?" Emil opens his mouth to speak but tears fill his eyes again. He glances at his mother, but she looks away overwhelmed. The officer waves at Emil as gesture to encourage him to speak and says soothingly "You are safe now". Emil nods, the officer presses in and ask, "Who did this to you?"

Emily and the other officers hold their breath as Emil inhales, wiping away his tears with his bloody hand.

"Tom. Tom Shaffer did it.", Emil speaks in terror.

"Okay. Who is Tom and where is he?", the police officer responds convincingly.

The sound of heavy footsteps is suddenly heard. Emily holds her breath, leaning against the door as several emotions battle within her. Her mind flashes to the wedding ceremony she had a few months back. She kissed Tom like she had no tomorrow, pouring into him all her fears and worries. He simply grinned at her, his eyes hungry. When his face comes into view, Emily sees the attractive bald man with sharp green eyes that she married. The female officer sees Tom walking down the stairs appears to be under the influence with no shirt, oil on his belly as she reaches for her gun on her belt; "let me see your hands".

Today, his monstrosity is evident. At the sight of the police officers, Tom's eyes widen in fear and then he looks over in a glare at Emily and Emil.

"What the fuck is going on here? Emily, why are pigs in my house? Who let them in?", Tom shouts aggressively.

Emily watches him in horror, tears streaming down her face. The police officer gets up and with powerful force, he grabs Tom by the neck and slams him to the ground. Emil scampers away to the safety of the female officer legs who is still holding her gun, her cheek gritted.

"You fucking piece of shit. That's a child! I'm going to kill you!", the blue eyed police officer speaks fiercely but Tom does not struggle with the officer. Instead, he lies limp on the ground underneath the officer who has fists ready to send a punch to his face.

"Stop!" The dark eyed officer yells, pulling the officer off Tom. Tom glares at Emil as the officers haul him up, handcuffs ready. Emil cowers against the female officer's legs.

Tom says, "I didn't do anything!" When the officers don't stop in their efforts to bind him, he chuckles loudly. "Are you taking the word of a nine-year-old? I didn't have sex with him. He is making it up."

"You have the right to remain silent, Mr. Schaffer," The dark eyed officer says into his face before pulling him along with him, the blue eyed officer who attacked walking behind them. Tom goes along but his eyes search for Emily everywhere. When he finds her, he gives her a grin and says to her with compassion "Baby, tell them that I love the kids like they were mine."

Emily opens her mouth, but the words barely make it out before the officers drag Tom out. Emily watches as they pull him towards their car, dragging him. Tom is saying something but they're not listening.

The dark eyed officer says loudly "Shut the fuck up and walk, Tom Shaffer, you are under arrest. Anything you say can be used against you in court. If you don't have an attorney and want one, one will be provided to you," before pushing Tom into the police vehicle and locking the door shut. Tom glances towards the house, his gaze connecting with Emily's.

CHAPTER 2

Flashback

A tired Emily walks into the salon, where she works part time after school, her bag trailing her. Like always, the salon smells of hair conditioner, nail polish, and the funny detergent Gina uses to clean the floor and the sound of women chattering.

Gina was saying animatedly to the women listening attentively to her "That was when I told him the truth. Look, honey, I'm not one of those sissy girls that you can use and toss, I mean business. You either ride and die for me or you get your tired behind out of my house!" That's Gina, a brilliant narrator and occasionally, a brilliant exaggerator but the girls never outed her secret.

"Hello," Emily says to the busy women who throw hellos over the heads of their customers. Emily settles into a chair, letting the cool air-conditioning hit her sweaty scalp.

"How was school, honey?" Gina asks and Emily nods, suddenly thirsty, rubbing her throat.

"School was fine. The usual learning, I suppose," she says casually, omitting the part about the usual bullying episodes she had to endure. She reaches for her bottle by her bag and gulps down the warm liquid while Gina chatters on, talking about her latest life escapade. Despite the rigorous work Emily has to do at the salon to make

some money for herself and her sick mother, she loves the time she spends here. It is the only time she barely remembers her sad life at home or her poor grades.

They are four girls. Gina is the head hairstylist. Being the oldest at the shop, she runs everything when Madam Agatha is out of town. She's also the prettiest. Flora once mentioned that Gina contested for Miss USA and she nearly qualified if it wasn't for her pregnancy. Gina is a brunette Barbie. Next in line is Missy. Missy is rather quiet like Emily and she only speaks a lot more when her husband, Frank, comes around. Gina often jokes that Frank is her talking drug. The twins, Helen, and Helena, are loquacious and chatty. Like Gina, they talk a lot but their escapades with men are what makes them famous in their small town. Madam Agatha, on the other hand, reminds Emily of an old spinster aunt who is hellbent on living and enjoying her life. She is often gone, a mistress to several men.

Emily is trying to pay attention to what the girls are saying when a knock on the salon door distracts them. A hush falls over the salon as Missy's husband walks in. Frank is gorgeous. Nearly everything about him is perfect and anytime Emily is asked to describe her dream man, she often thinks of Frank. Ordinarily, Frank's presence is greeted with a lot of excitement but today, the atmosphere is thick with tension. His hands are shaky as he stares at a quiet Missy.

"Hi, Missy."

Missy merely nods, not looking at him. Emily remembers her crying in the bathroom, telling them that Frank had slept with another woman. The twins were furious but oddly Gina, was the only one who was calm.

"Are you ready?" He asks quietly. Missy nods and Emily stares at her in shock. Two days earlier, Missy swore to never return to Frank and she was cheered on by the twins. Emily stares at the twins as they stay mute, their attention on the hair they're styling.

"Where are your things? Let me get them for you," Franks says sheepishly and Missy points towards Emily's chair where her suitcase is stacked. When Frank moves toward her, giving her a small smile, Emily refuses to move out of the way. Frank stares at her in confusion.

"Emily, darling, let the man get the suitcases."

"No," Emily finds herself saying. Gina's eyes widen as she stares at her. "She shouldn't go back. It's not fair!" Frank turns a bright shade of red as he scratches his hair in embarrassment.

"Emily..." There's a note of warning in Gina's tone but Emily doesn't budge. In one quick move, Gina strides over and with a surprisingly powerful force, pulls Emily out of the way and towards the backdoor. When they're finally outside, Emily turns to Gina, upset.

"But you told her to leave him!"

14

"Keep your Damn voice down!" Gina snaps, startling Emily. Gina never snaps. Gina is kind and nice and she never raises her voice.

Gina sighs, running a hand through her thick mane, "I know what the fuck I said, okay! And I changed it."

Emily feels her eyes welling up with tears, "But he cheated on her. He cheated," Emily whispers

Gina shakes her head and calmly says, "I know that but Emily, look at us. Me, you, Missy, Helen, and Helena. Which one of us came from a happy family? Emily, can you remember missing your dad and wondering where the hell he is?"

"What's your point?" Emely retorts.

"My point, Emily, is that we have to do whatever the hell we can to have what we didn't have as kids. Divorce isn't as sweet as it sounds, Emily and life is not a fairytale. Heck, men are shitheads," Gina chuckles as she reaches into her pocket for a cigarette. When she lights it, her face is contorted in anger.

"Life isn't a fairytale, Emily. Men cheat. All men cheat. They're so subsumed with sticking their fucking poles into whatever fucking space they can find like fucking animals. Note that, Emily. Any fucking hole." Gina pauses to blow a wisp of smoke in the air. "How old are you again?"

"Fourteen."

"Have you even had sex yet?" Emily shakes her head and Gina smiles, a hazy look on her face.

"Let me guess. You're saving it for someone special." When Emily does not respond, Gina snorts.

"Listen to me, honey. No boy out there is worth being called special. They'll sleep with you and then sleep with someone else afterward but here's where you've got to be smart for you and your kids should you decide to have any - you have to stay. Make it work. Do whatever the hell you need to do to be happy but don't let your babies grow up the way you did, with an absentee fucking father. Do all you can so your babies don't grow up without one."

****

Seated in her chair with her little bag on her lap, Emily watches with distant eyes as the doctor's fuss over her son. Weariness threatens to bring Emily's shoulders down, but she refuses to let it. There is no way she is going to crumble here. The ride to the hospital was long and silent. Emily can feel the cold stares of the doctors and nurses as they walk past her but she refuses to meet anyone's stare. If they have questions, they are simply going to have to come to her and ask themselves. Her hands are cold, but there is nothing she can do to heat them up. She lets her stomach rumble even though there's a vending machine opposite her. Her throat craves for something, but she doesn't know what it is, thirst? Hunger? or the emotions blocking her

16

airways, closing her throat preventing her from breathing. The doctors refused to let her into the examination room and without saying a word, she got the message they were trying to pass. They don't understand. They simply cannot understand. No one gets it and no one probably will and that's perfectly fine for Emily.

There's a wall clock above the examination room where Emil is. It's almost eleven and while her eyes are red from exhaustion, her body is perfectly alert. Her mind goes to her daughter, Lisa who is playing somewhere in the hospital's playroom. The thought of her daughter being violated is too hard to bear and Emily's mind immediately throws the thought out. Odd thoughts of Tom return and this time, they return with a vengeance. She remembers Tom's odd fascination with anal sex. She had found the act a little too weird but...No. It's all a lie. Her mind runs through memories of Emil being cold and distant from Tom.

He never really liked Tom. He was always waiting by the window on Sundays for his father and when Tom showed up in their lives, it took lots of coaxing to get Emil to be civil. Can Emil be paranoid? Or is this is another tactic to get Tom out of their lives? Emily sighs and lets these words run through her mind. It's another tactic and it can all be resolved if they can all get home together as one family.

There's a sudden vibration on her legs and Emily reaches for it slowly. Who could be calling at this time of the day?

Ivan. Emily stares at the ringing phone, afraid to pick it up. Her family is being threatened and if Ivan is calling to fire her for leaving, she simply would not be able to bear it. Her finger hovers over the icon before she finally clicks it. She can hear Ivan's breathing on the other end, but she doesn't say anything.

"Emily..."

"Ivan..."

"I heard. It's all over the news", Ivan initiates the convo. Emily sighs in relief but her body instantly tenses back up. If Ivan heard it on the news, then everybody else has probably heard it on the news as well. Emily winces, imagining what her gossiping neighbors must think.

"I was calling to apologize for keeping you at work so often. Also, Ivan voiced out with empathy. if you need some time away to be with your son, you need not worry. I've hired some waiters for the café," Emily stares at the vending machine, as she is trying to comprehend if there's a hidden meaning behind Ivan's words.

"Is this a nice way of telling me I've lost my job?", Emily replies sadly.

Ivan sighs. "No, Emily. I'm giving you time off to be with your family. You're free to come back whenever you're ready, okay?" Emily glances at the examination room's door, nodding. On the other end, she can hear the distant voice of a reporter on Ivan's TV. He's pitying her.

"I have to go, Ivan.", says Emily.

"My regards to your son.", Ivan ends the call. The door to the examination room opens and two doctors walk out. The female doctor speaks first, her expression blank.

"We've examined your son and he's alright now. We had to give him a few stitches and the bleeding has stopped. Thankfully, the injuries weren't any deeper than that. Your son also had some old scars in his anal region but again, it's only luck. The doctor with the blonde hair, Doctor Meryl, says "Your son's anal region could have been damaged beyond repair given the amount of abuse he has endured." Emily nods, wrapping her arms around herself.

The other doctor has a bottle of pills in her hand, "give him two of these, every morning for the pain. If he starts bleeding again, please bring him back in," the doctor says compassionately.

She further suggests "We'd like him to stay here tonight so we can observe him."

"I'd like to take him home," Emily says softly. The two doctors eye her with doubtful expressions.

"We believe it's pertinent for your son to stay here tonight," Doctor Meryl responds. Emily shakes her head, looking behind them at her son is lying on his chest on a bed.

"I want to take my son home," she says again. The second doctor looks irritated but is cautioned with a gaze by the other doctor.

19

"Alright then. We'll get the discharge papers ready." As the doctors walk away, the female officer from before appears in the hallway, another woman in tow, Emily thinks to herself.

"Mrs. Schaffer, this is Nancy Lopez. She's a child forensic interviewer and she is here to interview your son as is customary in child assault cases," says the female officer.

Emily nods, unable to speak as she gestures towards the examination room. The women walk in at once and Emily watches as Nancy puts on a big megawatt smile.

"Hi, Emil. I am Nancy Lopez, and I am a child forensic interviewer. I want to speak with you about what happened tonight. Is that okay?"

Emil glances at Emily and when she blinks, he responds. "Yes."

"Thank you, Emil, can you tell me what happened tonight?" She asks.

"My stepfather hurt me, two times" Emil replies.

"How? " She probes further.

Emil begins the story, and his voice fades out of Emily's ears as she finds herself unable to listen. Without another word, she bursts out of the room while Emil talks and leans against a cold wall. Gina's words echo in her ears, and she swallows the big ball of nausea that threatens to escape her throat.

"You, okay?" The female officer appears beside her. Emily nods as she fans her face.

"I'm sorry if this is hard but you have to be in the room while this is ongoing. Policy." Nodding, Emily takes in a deep breath to steady herself and thinks, "you can get through this, Emily."

****

At the Criminal investigation unit, Officer McConnell who is a desk police officer, sees detective Mesa walking in and with a smile states, "Welcome back, Detective."

Detective Mesa nods as he walks in. The entire day has been too stressful for him that he often joked about resigning, Yeah, yeah, this is my last one, he grumbles

The officer chuckled, shaking his head "You and I both know that's a lie, Mesa. You live for this," he exclaimed, and Mesa agreed. He lives for the thrill of it all. Detective Mesa walks into his office, towards his table where a small pack of burgers lies, uneaten. Sighing, he sits down, eyeing the lukewarm meal, he had forgotten to eat. This is why his first wife divorced him. She couldn't understand how he was always genuinely forgetting to eat and do things for her.

As he remembers what she often yelled at him, "But you never forget to reach for me when it's time to have sex," she yelled in his face a day before she moved her things out. He didn't stop her. Detective Mesa takes a bite out of the burger, and he groans as the mayo spills onto his mouth, mixing with the meat's juices. His stomach groans as he swallows and satisfies his two days hunger. That was very needed. His hands reach for a bottle of orange juice in a bag underneath his desk.

The unit is nearly empty, safe for two or three officers lurking around. For a small town, they have too many crimes but the officers never bother themselves beyond working hours, most of them are family men who constantly use their families as an excuse. As Detective Mesa chews thoughtfully, leaning back into his chair, his mind travels to the case for the evening. The kid whose face looked haunted upon their arrival. His bloody hands reminding him of a certain part of his childhood.

"Yo, Mesa! The child assaulter is in the questioning room. Chief wants you to handle it. The file is on your desk," a voice calls out and Mesa nods in response, his mouth full. The door of the questioning room is several steps away with an officer standing in front of the door, scribbling away. It takes Detective Mesa only a minute to consume the entire burger and orange juice. He grabs the file off his desk and makes his way to the questioning room.

"Detective Mesa," The officer says with a nod. He nods in return, having forgotten the officer's name. The room is dark, only lit up by a small bulb by the wall. It is equally sparse with only a table and two chairs. Tom Schaffer sits facing the door with a dark expression on his face and says

"You have no right to keep me here. I have a right to an Attorney!" Detective Mesa waves him off as he settles down into the chair opposite him.

"Yes, yes, but that right stops before our right to question you as well, Mister. I'd advise you to act accordingly so this can be short," Detective Mesa says as he glances into Tom's file. When he looks back up at Tom, his eyes are cold.

"So, you molested your stepson," Detective Mesa states.

"I did nothing of that sort," Tom replies.

Detective Mesa speaks to Tom "it says here that this is not the first time it happened. You have a penchant for sticking your penis into a small innocent children. Tell me, do you ever feel disgusted with yourself? Because you should. You are a disgusting animal."

Tom hits the table loudly, his eyes gleaming dangerously but Detective Mesa is unmoved, glaring back at him with so much hatred.

"You do not know anything about me," Tom growls.

Detective Mesa rolls his eyes as he reaches for a cigarette in his pocket. "Oh, yes. The customary 'you do not know anything about me' phrase. Do you know how many times I get that in a day, after questioning pigs like you?" He chuckles as he pulls out a lighter and lights the cigarette gently. Tom watches with hooded eyes as the Detective puffs a perfect ring into the air.

Here's the thing, dumbass. I do know a lot about you. For example, I know you were arrested for petty theft as a teenager. I know you've been charged with similar assault issues but miraculously, all the people who have charged you always deny the claims and recant. Need I go on?" Detective Mesa says in a quiet chilling voice. Tom's expression is blank, Mesa can see his heart beating wildly at the bottom of his neck. When he doesn't respond, Detective Mesa leans in and speaks assertively.

"You don't need to answer or say anything, I'm no asking you, I'm telling you. I know men like you. I see them every month, denying allegations, hiding behind a nice house and wife but deep down, you're nothing but dark, deranged psychopaths who dream and fantasize about terrible things. But guess what? You WILL be going to jail. You WILL pay for your crimes and the best part? There's going to be somebody behind those prison walls who will give you a taste of your own medicine."

Tom's face turns ashen and Detective Mesa watches as a drop of sweat rolls down his forehead. Satisfied to see Tom's fear, the Detective leans back, a triumphant glint in his eyes.

"So, I'm going to say the statement again and you're going to confirm it now so you and your attorneys could work a deal in your favor. You, Tom Schaffer, molested your stepson, Emil." There's a long moment of silence as Tom looks down, staring at his hands. The Detective watches him keenly, waiting. However, when Tom puts his head up, even though there's a cloud of fear behind his eyes, he is smiling at Detective Mesa.

"I know how this works. You say words to try to threaten me. I believe you, and then I say something I'm not supposed to say. At the end of the day, I am sent to prison. I'm not going to do that with you. Get me a damn lawyer," Tom says quietly. From the look in his eyes, he isn't going to budge. Detective Mesa rises slowly, his cigarette still in his mouth as he picks the file up. Turning around, Detective Mesa makes up his mind not to engage with Tom again.

"Oh, and Detective?" When Detective Mesa turns around to look at him, Tom is already on his feet. He leans out inches away from Mesa's face.

In a low unemotional murmur, he says, "I enjoyed every single moment I spent with that boy," He mouths out. A roaring sound fills Detective Mesa's ears and as he pulls back to hit Tom, a hand from behind stops him.

"Don't."

CHAPTER 3

The air in the courtroom is tense as Emily and her son walk in. Since the investigation at the hospital, Emil has gone quiet. This morning, his face is pale under the light in his blue shirt and dark jacket. Emily ignores the stares as they walk behind Mister Jones. He's the best they could afford. An image of an upset Tom comes to Emily's mind, and she exhales loudly. The sooner it starts, the sooner it will end. Emil is restless in his seat but Emily refuses to look at him, not after everything. Mister Jones is busy setting his documents ready on the table in front of them and up ahead, the court officials are just settling in. The judge's seat is however vacant.

Several minutes pass in the courtroom with everyone getting ready for the court session. When the officers bring Tom out, Emily rises to her feet. His skin is ashen, and his lips are set in a grim line. He scans the room quickly and when he finds Emily's eyes, her heart is racing wildly. A small sound escapes her lips. Tom's hands are handcuffed to a chain around his waist as he is placed in a chair. Tom sits within reach of Emily who reaches and touches his shoulder briefly. Tom stares at Emil, an unreadable look in his eyes, causing the boy to cower in his seat, looking terrified.

"Tom..." Emily starts but her husband simply looks away, his eyes suddenly dark. His chin is bushy and unkempt, giving him a wild look.

Tom says gruffly "The session is about to start," before turning to his lawyer. Tears prick the sides of Emily's eyes as the words she desperately wants to tell Tom are swallowed. She glances at Emil and her son quietly glances at her.

"All rise for the honorable judge, Elias Kenny," the court clerk declares loudly, and they all rise as a fat man with white hair, clad in his judge robes enters the room. It takes him a minute to settle his boisterous self into his seat.

"You can all sit," he says as he puts on his glasses. The atmosphere in the court shifts as the court officials settle, about to begin.

" The United States versus Tom Shaffer," The court clerk declares loudly. Emily watches grimly as the proceedings begin in full swing. The other lawyer opposite Mister Jones rises.

"Your honor. I'm Elizabeth Ricks on behalf of the US attorney's office." Elizabeth Ricks is tall with a long ponytail. Dressed fancily in a black pantsuit, she nods at the judge.

"I'm Matthew Jones on behalf of Mr. Shaffer."

Judge Kenny nods. "Welcome, attorneys to today's first preliminary hearing. Please call your first witness, Attorney Ricks."

"Your honor. The court calls Ms. Nancy Lopez."

Nancy Lopez takes the stand.

"Miss Lopez, kindly identify yourself and your title."

"I'm Nancy Lopez and I work for the Department of Child Advocacy as a Children forensic interviewer."

"Were you involved in an investigation that sequentially ended in the arrest of Mr. Tom Shaffer and do you see that individual here today?"

"Yes, and he is sitting to your right my left wearing an orange jumpsuit."

"Your honor, let the record reflect the in-court identification.

"Any objection?" Judge Kenny asks in attorney Jones' direction. He shakes his head respectfully.

"No, your honor."

"Very well. You may continue, Miss Ricks."

"Thank you, your honor. Ms. Lopez, can you relate to this court what your investigation revealed?"

"Of course, I interviewed Emil, the minor involved in this complaint, who stated that a few weeks ago, the defendant touched his genitals during shower time. The minor said that on multiple occasions, the defendant bathed his sister first and then him second. Emil said that, on more than one occasion, the defendant, Tom Shaffer, put his penis into the Juvenile's anus. Emil said that the incident first occurred when he was seven. Emil said that the defendant told him not to tell his mother or he would kill his mother. Emil said that the defendant would spread his butt apart and put his penis into his anus. Emil said that his rectum would bleed and hurt afterward. Emil described the defendant's penis as long and round. Emil said that the defendant's name is Tom Shaffer and is his stepfather. Emil said that the offense occurred inside his home of residence, in the bathroom.

Emil was given a diagram of a male and identified the penis as his private part. Lisa, who is Emil's younger sister, was interviewed at the Child Advocacy Center by me. Lisa said that the defendant touched Emil on his genitals. Lisa said that she observed the defendant doing it to Emil in the back one time. Lisa said that it was in the bathroom, and he yelled at her to shut the door. Lisa said that she observed the defendant putting his thing into her brother. Lisa said that Emil was on his stomach. Lisa said that the defendant was behind Emil. Lisa described Emil's private part as his pop hole.

Emil was shown a confirmation photograph of the defendant. Emil was asked about the person in the photo, and he replied, "That's my stepfather, Tom Shaffer, he hurt me." Emil made the positive identification.

Attorney Ricks nods. "Thank you, no further question.

Murmurings rise within the courtroom after Attorney Rick's statement. Emil, who is seated by his mother, begins to grow fidgety.

"I don't want to be here," He murmurs to himself whenever the judge looks at him. The judge appears like a kind man with kind eyes to Emil, but Emil does not trust anyone anymore. Not since Tom. He's never really liked Tom but his mom did. His mother appears to be in a world of her own, her gaze distant and unfocused. It appears as though she's listening to the proceedings, but Emil can tell she's distracted. He sighs, looking down at his hands.

"Mr. Jones, do you have any questions?" Judge Kenny asks; however, his face is blank.

"No, your honor. I'm Okay," Defense Jones says as he blinks at Tom who is clearly in distress. Tom looks backward at Emil, making him visibly frightened by Tom's gaze.

"Do you have additional witnesses, Miss Ricks?" Judge Kenny asks.

"No, you Honor. If we have no more questions from the defense, we will rest." Judge Kenny nods and points at Jones with his pen.

"Mr. Jones, do you have any witnesses?" The attorney nods as he rises with an air of importance. Instantly, Emil finds himself disliking the pompous attorney.

"Yes, your honor. The defense calls Miss Williams from Child Protective Services."

Miss Williams rises behind Emil's mother. She is dressed formally in a cream dress with a pearl necklace around her neck. Her dark heels echo in the courtroom as she makes her way to the stand. There, the court clerk approaches, raising one hand in the air.

"Do you swear to tell the truth, the whole truth and nothing but the truth so help you, God?

Ms. Williams nods solemnly. "I do."

"Proceed." Judge Kenny allows. Seated carefully, Miss Williams smiles at Emil, but Emil simply stares back at her, a hidden emotion behind his eyes.

"Good afternoon, Miss Williams and thank you for coming." Attorney Jones' voice is high and chirpy, a dramatic prelude to the information to unfold.

"Sure!"

"Miss Williams, can you please state your name and your employer?"

"Sure. My name is Beth Williams and I work for the department of Child Protective Services," she says calmly, eliciting a nod from him. With one hand in his pocket, the defense attorney inches forward toward her.

"Do you know Emil who is the complainant on this case?" Miss Williams smiles, glancing at him, aware of the Judge's gaze on her.

"Yes, Emil is a sweet and intelligent child. He is one---"

"Miss Williams, please answer the question," Jones interrupts, his voice suddenly hostile

Miss Williams is taken back, her shock evident. She turns to the Judge and the jurors.

"Ok but I need you to know that----"

"Miss Williams, once again, answer the question and nothing else. Your honor, can you please direct the witness to answer the question without any of her personal "beliefs" or interpretation of the complainant?" Jones snaps loudly. Judge Kenny's face remains impassive.

"Miss Williams, please stick to the questions."

Miss William's face turns red. "Okay. Sorry, your honor."

"Miss Williams, has Emil lied to you before?"

Miss Williams shakes her head, "he told me that he was scared and changed his story, but he is not a liar. He was scared of his stepfather."

Jones slams the paper he had picked up from his table hard. "Your honor, the witness is not following the court's direction and I move to erase her last statement from the record and instruct the jurors to disregard the last statement.

You honor permission to question the witness with hostility?" Jones asks. Miss Williams looks baffled; her mouth opens as murmurings rise again. Besides Jones, Attorney Ricks rises.

Judge Kenny sighs, rubbing his head. "Go ahead"

"Your honor, there is no need to..." Attorney Rick tries to interject but Judge Kenny turns his gaze on her, looking displeased.

"Miss Ricks, are you telling me how to run my courtroom?" Attorney Ricks looks defeated and sighs.

"No, your honor."

"Have a seat, counselor. Continue, Mr. Jones." Jones nods as he picks up the piece of paper from before again.

"Miss Williams, I have an email you sent to Emil's mother. It reads - I'm Beth Williams, a social worker who is investigating your son's case. Your son said to a friend in school that his stepfather hurts him while pointing at his buttocks, however, when I questioned him, Emil changed the accounts and told me that his story was all made up. As a matter of urgency, we must have a resolution to your son's interpretation of events. Can you please set a time to meet with me after school tomorrow? Is that the Email you sent Emil's mother asks Attorney Jones Miss Williams hesitantly responds "yes" So, I'll ask you again Miss Williams, did Emil change stories about the assault several times?"

Miss William's expression turns sad. She glances at Emil who has shrunk into his seat, with an equally sad expression on his face. The two stare at each other for a few seconds before Miss Williams finally looks away, her shoulders falling.

"Yes," she says quietly.

"So that's the definition of a lie, isn't it?" Jones asks, his voice loud and clear.

"Yes."

"No further questions. Thank you, Miss Williams."

Judge Kenny nods towards Ricks. "Do you have any questions, Miss Ricks?

"Your honor, can we have a brief recess?"

"This court is adjourned until two fifteen."

Emil watches as Miss Williams exits the stand and Judge Kenny makes his way out to his chambers. Miss Williams' face is withdrawn. She looks over at Emil and stares at his mother. The two women have a short stare down till Miss Williams finally looks away, shaking her head.

Emil swings his feet as he drinks from the box of juice a nice police officer gave him. Seated on a chair opposite the courtroom's door, he pays no attention to the people passing by casting glances at him. Instead, his gaze is fixed on the people inside the courtroom. From where he sits, he can see his mother and Tom, talking. His mother has her arm around Tom's shoulders while he talks, looking extremely displeased. His mother doesn't look upset with Tom. Instead, she's busy trying to calm him down, her hand moving across his shoulders in a placating manner. Emil's legs stop moving as he watches. Emil suddenly feels a presence beside him. Settling on the bench beside him is Miss Williams.

"Emil."

"Miss Williams."

The woman hands him a pack of chips and Emil gladly takes it from her, slightly hungry. The duo stared at Emil's parents and Miss Williams sighs.

"I'm so sorry, Emil," she says quietly. Emil stares back at her, quiet. The strict instructions his mother had given him earlier rings in his head about not to speak with anyone. With a final glance at the couple, Miss William rises and walks away. Emil stares at her retreating back, wanting to tell her thank you for the chips but the words die in his throat instead. Emil turns to face the courtroom and finds his view obstructed by Attorney Rick, Detective Mesa, and another familiar face, Nancy. Their conversation is muted but they keep glancing at Emil who stares back at them.

"Emil has to take the stand, or this case goes to shit! To tell you the truth, I'm not taking a loss," Ricks says in a hushed whisper to Nancy. Nancy glares at her, her face visibly upset.

"A loss? Ricks, Emil is a ten-year-old boy! A ten-year-old child, hurt by someone he trusted, his mother, and now us? Are you fucking crazy?" Nancy shoots back, risking a glance at Emil. Ricks sighs, running a hand over her forehead before pointing a careful finger at Nancy.

"My job is to make the case, to prove beyond a reasonable doubt. To win! I'm not going to lose my chance of becoming a supervisor or probably a fucking judge because of this kid, especially if he lied. I cannot appear incompetent defending a liar!" She says firmly. Nancy opens her mouth to speak but is unable to find the words, she looks at Detective Mesa who has remained quiet all through the argument.

Nancy asks him "Where do you stand?" Detective Mesa shrugs noiselessly and suggests, "Why don't we offer him a plea deal for less time and charge the mother for child negligence?"

"What?" Rick's pupils dilates but Detective Mesa is quick to put his hands up in the air.

"Hear me out, his little sister told his mother. She did not follow up. In spite knowing Emil was hurt, the mother did not call the police and attempted to prevent the police investigation during the initial report. Charge her and she may break. Maybe it will force her to see who this predator is when he pleads or even when he doesn't help her as she is helping him now. She is providing evidence to the defense." Nancy and Ricks share a look, pondering on Detective Mesa's words.

Detective Mesa says "Bottom line, we can't allow this kid to go through this. He is counting on us to protect him and I will." There is a short silence as the two women evaluate his words. Nancy is the first to agree to his words. Nodding apprehensively, she glances at Ricks.

"That's a good idea."

Ricks sighs, looking tired. "Let me call my supervisor."

They make way for Ricks who makes her way out of the courtroom. She glances at Emil who is still munching on his chips, his eyes following her every move. The attorney simply nods at him, her phone placed against her ears. Her words are barely understandable as she paces in circles, updating her boss. Emil glances back at his parents and he finds his mother smiling. A great feeling of anger and resentment wells up within him.

"Yes sir, I understand." Ricks is suddenly saying on the phone. When she turns around to face Emil, there's a grim look on her face. She tries to smile but the smile ends up as a grimace.

"Hey, kiddo. You're outside here all by yourself?" Emil nods as she settles down beside him. The attorney stares at him, making Emil feel slightly uncomfortable despite how nice she smells. She smells like his mother's favorite flowers.

"How are you finding the court proceedings? Fun?" Emil gives her a blank stare that causes her to laugh nervously as she rubs the back of her neck and lets out a tired breath.

"That's a dumb question. This isn't fun for you with your stepfather on the other side and you---well..." she trails off quietly. She glances at him again.

"What grade are you in?" Emil shakes his head, making the attorney's eyebrows go up in question.

"You're not in school? How's that possible?" She asks incredulously. Emil shakes his head again.

"I'm not allowed to talk to anyone," he says quietly, risking a glance at his mother who is still preoccupied with his stepfather. The attorney appears concerned for a brief second, but her face is suddenly readjusted into a blank canvas. She glances at Emil's mother and shakes her head.

"I wish you good luck, kid," she says with sincere eyes as she rises. "You're going to need it."

Puzzled by the attorney's queer remark, Emil chews his chips quietly as she slowly enters the courtroom. Emil realizes that people are returning to the courtroom. When his mother beckons for him, he simply obeys. There is no other choice. There is no other way.

CHAPTER 4

"All rise for the honorable Judge Kenny! This court is now in session!"

Emil returns to sit beside his mother, who now has a small smile on her face. Emil wants to grab her hand, but he restrains himself. Attorney Ricks is staring at Nancy and Detective Mesa, nodding quietly, as Judge Kenny sits. Looking replenished, Judge Kenny blows air out of his mouth.

"Miss Ricks, do you have any additional witnesses?" Attorney Ricks pauses as she rises to her feet, her expression grim. For a few seconds, she glances down at the documents on her table.

"Miss Ricks, I asked you a question." Attorney Ricks expels a soft breath.

"United States calls Emil." The courtroom explodes into loud murmurs as Attorney Ricks and other people turn to stare at Emil. Emil's heart suddenly begins to race as everyone's eyes get fixated on him. Worried, he stares at his mother and is terrified to find fear in her eyes. Now, he reaches for his mother's hand, terrified. Detective Mesa is visibly not pleased.

"Your honor, this is an outrage. That is a child!" Detective Mesa yells above the noise within the courtroom. Judge Kenny's face contorts in anger.

"Detective, take your seat and remain quiet or I'll hold you in contempt of court. Bailiff!" Detective Mesa stares at Judge Kenny with contempt, looking livid as he advances upon Judge Kenny.

"Contempt of court. Is that all you can do?" Detective Mesa sneers angered. Surprise is visibly written across Judge Kenny's face as well as the attorneys.

"Bailiff, remove the Detective from my courtroom and remand him for a day!" Judge Kenny yells as Detective Mesa keeps yelling, annoyed. Emil watches, terrified. What exactly is happening? US marshals walk to Detective Mesa and grab him by the arms. It's a wild scene as the Detective resists violently as he tries to pull away. His veins are visibly strained across his forehead as he points at Attorney Ricks and yells, "Emil is a child, a child who, like everyone is told to place their trust in us, THE SYSTEM!" Detective Mesa continues to yell and point at her "You betrayed him for your career, your career! You want society to trust the law? Trust the police? It doesn't matter what the law is or how good the police investigations are, because at the end of the day it's about wins for the prosecutors. You dismiss charges, put children on the stand because you don't want to "loose," you selfish bitch!" You don't care about the citizens, you only care about your stats. The Marshalls hold him in a tight grip, trying to haul him out. Attorney Ricks does not appear fazed. She stares back blankly at him.

"There is always another time, bro," One of the Marshalls, whispers against Detective Mesa's face hurriedly.

"Don't lose your job. Detective Mesa quiets down, a stony look on his face. As he passes Emil, Detective Mesa gives him a sad apologetic look.

"I'm sorry Emil," he says quietly before he is pulled out of the courtroom. Fear grips Emil tightly as the courtroom now falls quiet. Eyes follow Emil as he quietly makes his way to the stand. He glances at Attorney Ricks, who is unsmiling, and he shifts his attention to Tom. There's a dark vindictive look in Tom's eyes as he stares back at his stepson.

"Can you please raise your right hand and repeat this after me: I swear to say the truth and nothing but the truth, so help you, God?" The court clerk says loudly. Emil swallows heavily. He risks a glance at his mother and her apprehensive face scares him even further.

"Yes."

With a nod, the court clerk nods and gestures for him to sit. Attorney Ricks doesn't waste any time. She approaches the stand instantly.

"Emil..."

"Yes ma'am."

"Can you explain to the courts what you told Miss Lopez?" Quietly, Emil launches into an explanation, careful not to stare at his stepfather in the process. Attorney Ricks reassuringly nods as Emil continues to speak, making Emil feel more confident. When he's done, Attorney Ricks asks, "And you reported it to Ms. Williams the first time your stepfather hurt you, correct?" Emil nods. The Attorney sighs impatiently.

"Is that a yes?"

"Yes."

"And then later, during the interview you took it back, correct?"

"Yes, because I was scared." Attorney Ricks folds her arms, putting one leg out.

"Scared of what exactly? Of getting discipline for lying or because something was going to happen to your mother?"

Defense Jones springs up instantly. "Objection! Your honor, she is putting words in his mouth."

Judge Kenny says "Sustained. Miss Ricks, ask him another way or change the question."

"Very well, your honor. Emil, why were you scared?"

"My stepfather said that he would kill my mother if I told."

Murmurings rise within the courtroom at Emil's statement. Even Attorney Rick's face changes slightly but she quickly puts on a blank mask.

Attorney Jones shouts, objection you honor, my client is not being charged with threats, it's irrelevant.

Attorney Ricks says you honor I'm trying to establish…

Judge Kenny interrupts, "I will allow it."

Attorney Jones displeased states, very well you honor.

Attorney Ricks, continues "Emil did you believe your stepfather when he said that he would kill your mother?" More murmurings rise within the courtroom.

"Yes."

"No further questions for this witness."

Judge Kenny nods. "Mr. Jones, your witness." Defense Attorney Jones rises, looking excited.

"Thank you, your honor, he looks at Emil and asks "Emil, has your mother hit you in the past?"

"Objection, that is irrelevant." Attorney Ricks interjects.

Attorney Jones responds "Your honor, this witness was not on the list, to begin with, and Miss Ricks is questioning past hearsay and something that my client is not being charged with. So, I need some latitude to show the motive and background of this frivolous investigation."

"I will allow it. Overruled. Continue."

"Has your mother hit you in the past?"

Emil nods "yes but she didn't mean to, and it was not hard."

Attorney Jones Asks Emil so are you saying it was not hard or she didn't mean to hit you, which is it, Emil.

Emil is confused and is not sure how to answer and he says, "umm It was, she didn't mean to hit me"

Attorney Jones then asks Emil, are you trying to protect your mom?

Emil responds no.

Attorney Jones asks, "Have you ever lied?"

Emil says "No." Attorney Jones quickly retorts, but Emil are you not lying to me now about your mom hitting you?

Attorney Ricks Quickly objects and says he is badgering the witness.

Judge Kenny, lets out a sigh and says Mr. Jones is this going somewhere? Attorney Jones says yes, your Honor, I'm getting there.

Judge Kenny says, "Overruled."

Attorney Jones continues, Okay. Emil, is it a fact that you told Miss Williams that your stepfather didn't allow you to go out and play and that you didn't like him because of this? Emil's face turns cloudy as he suddenly begins to stutter.

"I-I-I did."

"And is that the reason why you made up the touching and the hurting?" Jones pushes, eliciting murmurs within the courtroom. Emil's face turns red as he shakes his head vigorously.

"No, he hurt me," Emil cries, suddenly feeling overwhelmed. Defense Jones shakes his head dramatically, glaring at Emil with a disappointed look.

"But you lied, right? You said that it happened, then you said that it didn't, when in fact it didn't happen" right? Tears begin to build within Emil's eyes as he tries to understand what the attorney is driving at.

"Yes but…"

Attorney Jones does not wait for Emil to finish and continues, "So, you did lie then, as you are doing now. You are willing to hurt your family and tear it apart with a lie!" Jones says loudly, his voice increasing in volume. His words strike a chord within Emil, as he remembers what his mom told him *"Tom gives everything to us, our lives have changed since I met him!"* When he glances at his mother, he finds no help. She stares back at him, her eyes sharp, though glistening with tears, feeling alone, Emil breaks down.

"Mommy, tell him to stop---," Emil wails as he wipes his wet eyes stubbornly. Emily nods at him as he cries. Emily says "tell them the truth, baby. Tell them the truth," Emily says softly as tears stream down her own eyes. At the sound of her voice, Emil looks up at her, and sees his mother's unspoken pleading in her eyes.

"Don't look at your mom. Look at me! Tell me the truth!" Jones screams startling Emil who simply cries further.

"I lied! I lied! Sorry, I lied!" Emil yells back, causing the courtroom to descend into a collective gasp of disbelief. Low conversations ensue as Emil sobs in his seat.

"Please stop," He whispers but no one hears him.

"Your honor, I move to dismiss all charges against my client without prejudice," Jones says with boldness and Judge Kenny leans back into his chair. With one glance at Emil, Judge Kenny nods and says "I agree, he looks over at Ricks, and asks, Prosecution?"

"The Government rests." Says Ricks and glances at Tom, her face withdrawn.

She non emotionally says in a flat voice "Sir, you are free to leave. Have a great day and my deepest apologies for this ordeal." Judge Kenny announces "This court stands adjourned" before banging his gavel loudly.

In a quick move, Tom gets up and rushes towards Emily who receives him with a warm embrace and a kiss. Tom attempts to hug Emil's sister who had joined the proceedings towards the end, but the girl pushes him back in fear.

Emil still sitting on the stand, sobs loudly, dejected. Nancy Lopez rushes to Emil, tissues in her hands.

"Why are they so mean? You promised!" He cries at the woman, but no one responds.

No one answers.

At the welcome back home gathering, Tom is heard saying "It was all a big misunderstanding, I assure you!" while Emil seated watches from the corner of the house. Since the case was dismissed, Tom set out on a making-things-right spree. Many of the neighbors heard about his arrest and they were all skeptical about having Tom back in the neighborhood. There were even rumors that the neighbors were all planning to have Emily and Tom evicted from the neighborhood. In a panic, Emily and Tom set out to pacify their concerns. Tom was still refusing to let Emil go out to play with the other kids. Tom used the excuse, "He might try to spread more lies, let's just leave him to play indoors." His mom agreed swallowing every word Tom said like a fish taking bait.

"But we heard that there was evidence. Your stepson had injuries in his backside, Mister Schaffer. Surely, you can see why we would be worried," One of the neighbors, Mrs. Thompson, says, sitting extremely close to her husband. Her eyes dart from Tom to Emily, casting a furtive glance on them. There are about ten different neighbors in their small living room and Emily, a brilliant host, had made more than enough food to go around but the neighbors were barely touching it.

"Oh, there were some injuries, but it wasn't caused by Tom," Emily interjects with a nervous smile. "Emil has a bad habit of playing with sharp objects and honestly, we don't even know how it happened because neither of us was there, but we assume he sat on one."

"I don't know, Emily. Your boy behaves rather strangely. When we heard the news, it kind of made us understand him. No offense, Tom," Mister Rodriguez says as he reaches for some chips. His wife, Lily, smacks his arm and he blushes in embarrassment.

"My apologies."

"Oh, none was taken. Look, guys, Tom says, I understand that this is difficult for you to believe but let's look at it from the angle of the law. Would a Judge, in his right mind, acquit a man who is a sexual offender? Come on, think about it! The only reason, I am here is that I am innocent and that there simply was no case. Come on, guys. Let us think about that for a brief minute," Tom says charismatically as he takes a swig out of his beer. For the occasion, he's dressed in his favorite blue shirt and sturdy brown pants, the ones Emily says make him look responsible. It was his idea to bring all the neighbors together. While Emily barely cared for their opinions, Tom could not stand being castigated. When the neighbors in the living room fall quiet, pondering on Tom's words he takes Emily's hands into his.

"I love this woman with all my heart," He begins softly with a small smile. "I always have from the moment I met her, I knew instantly that I was going to marry her. And I did!" He exclaims, leaning in to place a big kiss on her lips. When he withdraws, for a split second his eyes glaze with the malevolence Emil has seen before, but it goes unnoticed by everyone else.

"As beautiful as our little family is, little Emil hasn't exactly taken it in good faith. I mean, what child wants to see another man take the place of his father? It's natural to be antagonistic. It's what little children do." A couple of neighbors nod in agreement and Tom, seeing that he is gaining ground, shakes his head sadly.

"All I've ever wanted was a big and happy family. I understand that it's taking a while for it to sink in for little Emil, but I trust that it will. I'm willing to do whatever it takes." He shrugs. "It's a pity that little Emil would succumb so low and say such a foul accusation against me. I've done nothing but love and care for him since the day I met him."

Tom looks in the direction of Emil and the boy cowers in his chair. Though Tom is all smiles, Emil can see the daggers in his eyes and the message he is trying to pass across. You better cooperate with me.

"He's right," Mister Thompson says, speaking up for the first time. "When my mother got married again, I used to pour sand into my stepfather's shoes. For some reason, I thought it would work because the man hated the sand in the house." The adults chuckle, easing the tension they all brought in earlier.

"I remember dating a single Dad once and his girls would swap out my shampoo for dog cream," Natasha, another neighbor opposite the Thompson says, nodding her head.

Tom chuckles loudly, "I really can't blame any kid who does that. They simply just do not want a replacement. Kids barely understand things like love and companionship.

Emily adds softly, "We're having conversations with Emil to make it better and easier for him. Lisa has adjusted fast", and the neighbors nod in accordance.

"Perhaps you should consider therapy. You all could go as a family to unburden and unpack," someone chimes in, and one by one, the neighbors offer words of advice, which Tom and Emily take with grand smiles.

In the corner of the kitchen where Emil is seated, a sleepy Lisa walks in with her doll tucked carefully underneath her armpits. "Emil? I cannot sleep. They're making too much noise," She whispers to him. Her quiet brother pulls her into the chair with him and lets her lay her head on his chest. With his arm around her, he rubs her back carefully as he has seen his mother do.

"Emil, are you sad? Because I am." Emil shakes his head, unwilling to let his sister see his sadness.

"Don't be sad, Lisa. I will be fine. We will be fine."

Though Emil mutters those words softly, he does not believe it.

CHAPTER 5

Leaves crumble underneath Emil's feet as he runs as fast as he can. The sky is dark, and the wind seems to be against Emil, moving loudly against his ears as it tries to slow him down. Emil cries out in fear, and he glances back. He needs to run faster. Emil doubles up, running with all his might but he doesn't get far. A hand grabs him by the waist, and another covers his mouth to stop him from yelling. Emil struggles, screaming against the enclosed and smelly hand but no one can hear him. Slowly, he is dragged back into the house. Unable to bear it anymore, Emil forces his eyes open, gasping for breath as he stares around the quiet room for any possible attack, but none is in sight.

Sighing, Emil lies on his bed, his eyes vacant as he stares at the door. His neck glistens with sweat despite the cool breeze that saturates the room. It's been two days since the court case and nightmares have been plaguing his dreams even during the day. There are so many characters in the dreams - Detective Mesa, Nancy, Attorney Ricks, his mother, and the villain - Tom. The nightmares take different forms, but the content is the same. Despite the conversations, he has with the other people in his dreams; he still ends up in Tom's hands. The thought terrifies Emil more than anything in the world.

When they returned from the courthouse with Tom in tow, his mother called for a small family meeting where Tom told his barefaced lies again and his mother gulped them up. Since then, Tom has been staring at him with a dark emotion behind his eyes, and more than ever, Emil wanted his freedom. His eyes watched Tom's every movement and as much as Emil hated being stuck in his room, Tom kept ordering him to remain there. Emil glances at the ground to see if little Lisa was still playing with her toys. Lisa is however not there. Emil starts to panic. The thought of Tom hurting his sister is unbearable.

Emil rushes towards his window and manages a breath of relief when he spots Lisa outside, playing on the lawn. Lisa must not be touched. The sky outside is equally dark as in Emil's dream. Emil wants to call Lisa in but decides against it. She should play outside till his mother arrives.

Emil returns to his bed, sighing. There must be something he can do to prove Tom's evil nature. The door suddenly bursts open, startling Emil. Staggering in is a slightly drunk and shirtless Tom. Emil swallows as his pulse beats even faster. His nightmare has finally come for him. Tom glares at him, holding a bottle of whiskey in one hand as he slowly closes the door behind him. Emil flies off the bed and inches against the wall, his hands cupping his privates. The sight of a terrified Emil causes Tom to cackle loudly as tears bloom in Emil's eyes.

"I told you they would never believe you!" He snarls, shaking the bottle dangerously in front of Emil, glaring at him with a face full of rage and malice. Emil shakes his head as Tom advances on him. "I'm not going to cry," Emil says within himself but a traitorous tear escapes.

"No. Please, no, I won't tell anymore," Emil says softly as Tom throws the bottle of whiskey against the wall and grabs Emil with such force that the boy hits the sides of the bed and falls back. Emil cups his privates, ready to shiver.

"No. Please, no!" Emil begs but Tom moves with infuriated force. He hits Emil sharply across the face and the boy's neck snaps to the other side. Emil whimpers as Tom pins his hands under his knees and unzips his shorts. The sound of his zipper causes Emil to suddenly begin to sob again.

"No. Please, no, I won't tell anymore!" Emil cries.

Out on the lawn, Lisa hears the distant and familiar sound of Emil's cries. Worried for her brother, she hurries into the house and heads straight for his door, but she finds it closed. Her heart races as she remembers Emil's words. Never enter the room whenever Tom is doing bad things to me, okay? Emil made her promise. Lisa runs outside again, sad as tears grow within her eyes. Tom is always doing bad things to Emil. Lisa sits on the steps in front of the house and listens to her brother's cries. Her toys remain untouched on the lawn, and she wonders if her brother will ever be able to play with her anymore.

The wind blows softly against Lisa's hair as stars begin to appear in the sky. Lulled by the wind, Lisa leans against the pillar and dozes off. It's about ten minutes later that Lisa awakes to a hand shaking her thoroughly. When she opens her sleepy eyes, her mother is looking down at her, confused.

"Why aren't you asleep?" she asks. Lisa blinks, taking a few seconds to get her bearings then she finally realizes it's her mother. Lisa frantically says "mommy, Tom is hurting Emil again. You must help him!"

Emily sighs in exasperation. "Now you too, Lisa?"

"Mommy please, he's with Emil, in the room! The door is locked!" Lisa says with wide eyes.

Emily stares at the door to her house, her thoughts running wild. All this time, she believed Tom over her kids... This can't possibly be true. The distant sound of her son crying calls out to Emily. With one glance at Lisa, Emily takes a cautious step up the stairs and into the house. The living room is vacant and dark, but she can hear movements from Emil's room. With each step that she takes, her heart beats louder and louder as she inches closer to the locked door. Gently, she tugs on the handle, but it refuses to give way.

From within, she can hear the familiar grunting of Tom, the same grunting that he makes atop her. Feeling very helpless, she suddenly turns around and runs downstairs as she breathes loud. The kitchen is bright, but her confusion and panic make what she's searching for more difficult to find. It takes her nearly three minutes to reach for the huge knife hidden at the far end of her kitchen cabinet. Running back upstairs, Emily tugs on the door. When it doesn't give way, she gets to work, hacking the lock as best as she can.

55

When the door finally splits open, the horrifying sight causes the knife to slide out of her hands as she covers her mouth in horror. Emil is curled up in the fetal position complexly naked and mute as he stares back at his mother, his eyes vacant. Tom is asleep on the bed in all his naked glory with his bottle of whiskey in shatters by the wall where he threw it earlier. Tom's thighs have white streaks of a familiar fluid.

Staggered Emily reaches for the blanket on the floor, and with careful hands; she wraps Emil and carries her son up and out of the room. Emil barely says anything as Emily rushes him out of the room, her tears now pouring freely. Emil doesn't respond as she carries him into the living room. Lisa is seated on the couch, her small eyes widening as she sees them.

"Baby, grab me my phone," Emily sobs as she places Emil down on the rugged floor. "Baby, what happened? Talk to mommy. What happened?" Emil finally seems to see her but the look in his eyes petrifies Emily to her core.

"Nothing happened, Emily. It's all a lie," Emil says in a voice devoid of emotion. Lisa appears beside Emily, handing her the phone. Emily dials 911. She barely gets through the call; she is crying so much it's hard to understand her.

"I'm sorry, Emil. I'm so sorry," She whispers as she cradles him until the officers arrive. She's unable to hear or see them till she hears someone speaking.

"Take her too. Lock her ass up."

Hands reach for her, pulling her away from Emil. A strangled cry fills the air as they take Emil away from her and she fights them tooth and nail, but they are too strong for her. They deposit her beside Tom inside the cruiser and Emily weeps as the car drives her away, further and further away from her babies.

CHAPTER 6

Twenty years later

The weather is cool but that does not matter to the man jogging across the streets. Sweat sticks to his armpits and rolls across the front of his tank top as he increases his pace. He pauses occasionally to glance at the watch on his left hand. He's been jogging for nearly thirty minutes even though his muscles scream for relief, he has a target. Besides, he is no stranger to pain. He has never been. The sun is rising behind the clouds, casting an orange glow across town and he smiles, remembering the promise his son made the other day. *I'm not going to sleep, Dad. I'm going to stay awake till the sun comes up.* Barely two hours later, his curly-haired son slept off in his arms, sprawled in a wild position. He, however, was unable to sleep, troubled by the familiar ghosts of his past so he watched the sun come up, his son safely tucked against his chest.

Five minutes later, target accomplished, the man finally pauses his jogging, taking his time to breathe and stretch his aching muscles. As he stretches, he observes his environment. Within the houses along the street, people are just rising from their sleep and the silence on the street is occasionally punctuated by the sound of metals clashing against one another from someone's kitchen or the sound of a car starting. There's the occasional distant yell from an exhausted parent and the cry of a child unwilling to go to school.

Slowly, the man begins to make his way back to his house. His nightmares have returned, leaving him more tired than he was when he runs. Running however helps. It has brought him more comfort and joy than he could have ever imagined. He wouldn't have met his wife if he wasn't taking his morning run across the streets of the college where she attended. She often jokes that he would have thrived as an athlete and he always laughs along, unwilling to tell her that, he runs because he is afraid of his nightmares. He nods at a neighbor who is washing his car across the street. The neighbor from down the street waves vigorously, a wet washcloth in his hands. Occasionally as he approaches his house, cars move past the him, and he takes his time to peer closely at each one like a lion watching the gazelle, taking in every detail.

Despite being only steps away from his house, the walk home takes another ten minutes. His house is a small green house with a white picket fence and a wide lawn. His wife had been rather insistent on the type of house she wanted, and he obliged her. There are flowers by the edges of the fences which his wife takes time to cultivate. The concrete path leading up to the front porch is littered with miniature action figures. The man makes a mental note to put all the toys in the garage later.

The house is quiet as he steps in, sweating slightly. Like the lawn, the living room is littered with shoes and books. It's a beautiful room with bright yellow walls and cream furniture, one of which has a grey cat on it. Meowing loudly, the cat watches as the man inches towards the window and glances out of it. His mind begins to unfurl and slowly, he begins to recite all the tags of the vehicles he saw on his run. There's a small board with markers hanging on the wall, by the window. He moves towards the board and dutifully writes down the vehicle tags. Lost in thought, he continues, oblivious to the sound of footsteps approaching.

"Good morning." he however doesn't hear the voice, his mind is cloudy and fixed on what he is doing.

"Emil, are you listening to me?" The voice says loudly and he, startled, turns around. Staring at him through green eyes, is Caitlyn, his wife. Her blonde hair falls in waves around her pretty face. Dressed in a green shirt and a black bandage skirt, Caitlyn looks stunning and Emil notices, smiling widely.

"I'm so sorry, baby. I was daydreaming," he says as he moves in and kisses her softly, his hand around her waist. Caitlin smiles and says "Baby, wake up the kids. I don't want them to be late again, okay?" Emil nods as he kisses her cheek.

"See you tonight at dinner. Love you," She hugs him and begins to make her way out the door.

"Okay but I'm taking a shower first. And love you more!" He yells as she leaves the house, closing the door gently behind her. Sighing, he looks away as the distant sound of her greeting their neighbors reaches his ears. Emil glances out the window to watch as she leaves. The cat meows again and Emil stares at it. The lazy stretching cat stares back. After a quick shower, he thinks to himself, time to wake the kids up.

His children's room is an explosion of art and childish ingenuity. Since they were old enough to speak, the children refused to sleep in separate rooms. Instead, they share a bed and a room. Emil stands at the door, watching the sleeping duo. A distant memory is brought to mind, but Emil pushes it down quickly, fighting any old feelings of nostalgia. Emil Junior has one hand across Paola's face, drool running out the side of his mouth while Paola's legs are sprawled across Emil Jr's stomach. The sight brings a small smile to Emil's face. How the two manage not to fall out of the bed every night is unfathomable. Gently, Emil heads over and shakes their legs.

"Junior, wake up, son. It's a school day." Junior groans as he turns in bed, ignoring his father.

"Paola, wake up, baby. It's time for school," Emil shakes her leg. Paola yawns and stretches loudly as she opens her eyes. For a few seconds, looking tired, she stares hazily at her father. Emil smiles, waiting, waking Paola up is never difficult. Junior, on the other hand, is another case entirely.

"Okay, Dad," Paola mumbles as she rubs her eyes, rising slowly. Junior's butt is still upturned in the air as he stretches, refusing to get up. Emil smacks his son's butt softly and the boy groans.

"Can't we stay home today?" He murmurs and Paola makes a sound in agreement, nodding vigorously. Emil laughs as he pulls Paola up.

"No, you can't. While you're under my roof, you simply must get an education. It's an absolute must."

"Education sucks," Junior whines.

Emil shakes his head. "You've got fifteen minutes to get ready and you better be ready." Emil is about to leave the room when he feels warm hands wrap around his waist. From the gentle grasp, he can tell that it's Paola. Carefully, he twists and hugs her back, making sure to kiss her on her head.

"Love you," He murmurs into her hair.

After getting dressed and a hefty breakfast, Junior shouts "Dad, the school bus is here!"

Emil, whose hands are buried under soapy water, glances over his shoulder to see Junior running out of his room, holding his backpack and a cellphone in his hands.

"Okay, love you! And don't get caught with the phone again, okay?"

"Okay! Love you too!" Junior yells as he slams the door behind him. Emil sighs as he rinses the last plate. Whoever said taking care of kids is a small feat need to be smacked. Behind him, Paola is busy chewing her cereal loudly. Emil glances at the watch around his hands.

"Baby, are you done? We're going to be late if you don't hurry up!" The loud noise of a chair scraping the floor reaches Emil's ears.

"I'm done eating, Dad. I'll go pack now!" Paola's bare feet slap against the ground as she dumps the cereal bowl in the sink in front of her father, before he could reach for it and runs away.

"Paola, this is not what we discussed now!" Emil chuckles loudly as he reaches for the small bowl. Paola hates doing dishes and Emil has been trying to get her to at least, always do her dishes. Emil quickly washes the bowl, listening to Paola's movements in her room.

"Paola, are you ready? We have to go!" Emil calls out as he wipes his hands with a napkin and grabs his keys off the kitchen table. He glances at his wristwatch again, fifteen minutes to eight.

"Almost done," She yells as she runs into the kitchen with her shoes on and her backpack on. Her eyebrows are furrowed in concern as she stares at her father.

"Have you seen pretty?"

Emil shakes his head as he puts one hand out for her backpack. "No, she is probably outside."

"I need to feed him, Dad." Emil sighs noiselessly. Paola will not make another move unless she feeds Pretty, her cat. Emil makes a mental note to have Pretty locked up every morning after his morning run.

"Look outside, baby." Paola dashes outside through the backdoor and goes looking for Pretty while Emil looks for his phone. Paola's teacher will have one or two words to say about her late arrival again. Emil shrugs as he walks into his bedroom, looking for his phone. It takes him about a minute to find the phone buried under his blanket. Shaking his head, he makes his way outside. If they don't leave in the next minute, they'll be too late.

"Paola!" Emil calls as he steps onto the porch. Paola is nowhere on the lawns and Emil sighs. Why are kids like this?

"Paola!"

Emil walks back into the house and scans the living room and then the kitchen. It's empty. Emil pauses before heading out of the kitchen through the backdoor. Their backyard is wide and without a fence, merely partitioned by wild bushes and trees. Paola is still nowhere in sight. Emil ventures further, searching underneath the branches of the trees.

"Paola, if this is a scheme so you won't go to school, I can assure you it's not funny," Emil calls out, searching. Even Pretty is nowhere to be found. Sighing, Emil goes back into the house and checks Paola's bedroom. Her toys are on the ground, but the room is devoid of her presence.

"Paola!"

Emil yells as he begins to check the bathrooms and the other rooms. Panic hangs at the back of his mind, waiting to be let out in full force. Emil bursts out on the front porch again, examining the lawn. This time, he spots the mailman by the side of their mail post. Emil runs down the walkway, panting.

"Sir, have you seen my daughter? Brown hair, 5'5', slim, wearing a school uniform?" The mailman looks irritated by the disturbance. He gives Emil a once over. He shakes his head.

"Nah bro, I haven't seen anyone out here."

Emil watches in panic as the mailman walks away. He glances down the street but there's no sight of Paola. Emil's chest threatens to burst with panic as his breathing increases and his hands turn sweaty. A sound catches his attention, and he looks around for the source. It's coming from his neighbor's house. Occasionally Pretty has gone over to play with the neighbor's cat, Jingles. Emil runs to the neighbor's house and knocks on the front door frantically. When the door pulls open, Emil is in full panic mode.

"Ben, have you seen Paola? She is not in the house or outside!" Ben is a middle-aged Caucasian man with a bald head and a big stomach. Ben looks concerned as he steps outside to join Emil on the porch.

"Calm down, take a breath Emil. I haven't seen your little girl at all today." Emil exhales loudly, running a hand through his hair as terror kicks in. Where is Paola? He just saw her walking out the door.

Ben says soothingly Emil "You know, juveniles. She is probably on the way to school because she wants to walk with a boy and doesn't want to be embarrassed by her parents." the words lower Emil's panic level a bit, Emil nods and replies that's possible, Caitlin did say the other day, that Paola has a crush on some boy in the neighborhood. Please keep an eye open, I'll be right back."

Ben nods vigorously, "Sure thing." Emil rushes off to check the house again, his pulse-pounding. After scouring for a few minutes, Emil stands on his lawn, his arms akimbo, as he tries to regulate the frenzy within himself. Ben's words return to him, and Emil makes a decision. He walks fast towards his car. If Paola has indeed found her way to school, he needs to make sure that she is at school.

"God, please," Emil whispers as he gets into the car, igniting the engine at once.

"Damn it!"

Emil yells at a driver as he swerves sharply. The driver yells and curses at Emil, but he barely hears it, and continues zooming off. Paola's school is a five-minute drive from the house, but Emil reaches the school in less than three minutes. Despite his crazy driving, his gaze moves from left to right, looking for Paola's familiar physique but the streets are void. The school gates are open, and, in a hurry, Emil parks his car by the sidewalk before leaping out towards the school gate.

The school gate is open but there are no students outside, a sure sign that school has begun. Emil rushes in and is greeted by a swarm of kids in the hallway. His brain buzzes panic words loudly as he moves around, trying to spot Paola's class.

The door to her class is open and he finds her teacher, Miss Davenport, seated, going over her notes.

"Hello, Mister---"

"Miss Davenport Emil interrupts, is Paola here? The teacher appears surprised as she takes in Emil's rattled appearance. She rises slowly, shaking her head.

"No, I haven't seen her yet, sir." Before she can utter another word, Emil rushes out back into the hallway where students are already trooping into their classrooms. That's when he sees the familiar bobbing head. Rushing towards him, he yells her name. She turns around and greets with a polite smile on her face, freckles scattered across her face.

"Tiffany!" Emil gasps. "Have you seen Paola?" Tiffany shakes her head, looking confused.

"No, sir. Why?" Emil lets out a shaky breath, feeling his fingers vibrate as he tries to calm himself.

"I can't find her." Tiffany stares blankly at him, not understanding. Emil tries to find more words to explain but how can he tell anyone that one minute, Paola was with him and the next, she simply wasn't?

"Does she have a boyfriend, a boy she likes, or anything like that, please tell me the truth?" Emil asks desperately as the crowd in the hallway thins. Tiffany shakes her head again.

"No, she is not into boys. All she does is draw her cat, pretty."

Pretty! he repeats, as realization hits and he remembers she was looking for Pretty. With a final nod at Tiffany, Emil walks away, mentally running through his movements for the past thirty minutes. She was searching for Pretty and he made sure to check the backyard... or did he? He second guesses himself. As Emil makes his way out of the school, he glances at the sky and prays to himself, please let this be a dream. Let me return home to find Paola. Let it be a prank or a misunderstanding. All through the drive home, Emil clutches the steering wheel tightly, at the edge of his seat.

"Paola is home. Paola is home," Emil chants under his breath as he drives carefully this time, trying to reign in his panic.

The house was just as he left it and this time, Emil takes measured steps into the house to search with a new perspective. Slowly, he goes through the checklist in his mind. The living room is empty. The kitchen is empty, but

Emil does not relent. He mindlessly pulls open all the cupboards and drawers carefully.

"Paola, baby, please," Emil mutters as he descends into the basement, searching thoroughly. His panic increases as he moves around until he is finally in the backyard, searching underneath trees and branches. Breathing slowly becomes difficult as Emil's throat becomes choked with fear. A wave of nausea washes over him as he ventures deeper into his backyard, tears building in the corner of his eyes. When Emil finally emerges out of the bushes, his face is red.

"Did you find the girl?" A voice interrupts his search and Emil glances up, his face wet with tears. Ben is standing in his backyard, watching Emil.

"No. Ben, I don't know where she is!" Ben heaves, his shoulders slumping as he takes in the tired man

"Call the police. I heard in the news that there is a maniac loose and kidnapped three young girls," Ben delivers quietly, looking sullen.

Emil's hands fly to his mouth in horror. "Oh my god! Oh, my Godddd!" Emil begins to weep, his hands over his head as he falls into shock.

"What am I going to do? What am I going to tell my wife? She was literally just here. I swear to God that I just saw her!" Emil cries as Ben approaches him. The man puts a hand on his shoulder.

"You're going to need to be strong, Emil. If she was truly taken by this maniac, you're going to need all the faith and courage you can muster," Ben says calmly as he puts his hand out. Emil takes it and lets him pull him up.

"Your wife is not going to take this news lightly. You must be strong, for her and your son, Jr." Emil nods, wiping the snot that's rolling down his nose.

"I have to be strong," He repeats, shaking his head. Ben nods alongside, tapping Emil's arm.

"You have to be strong," Ben repeats.

It takes Emil a minute to regain composure as he stares up into the sky, blinking back every tear that has formed in his eyes. Ben supports him to stand, waiting dutifully.

"Come on, let's go into your house. Let's go call the police," Ben nudges as he pulls Emil along. Broken, Emil follows as the terrible thoughts of the maniac run through his head.

CHAPTER 7

Images of Paola tied and gagged suddenly causing a feeling of nausea in Emil. "I wish I could just throw up, so I can feel better," Emil whispers in a low tone. Unable to help himself, Emil yanks his hand out of Ben's and vomits profusely into the grass. Ben rubs his back gently as Emil spills his guts out, tears running down his face.

This is his worst nightmare.

Ben settles Emil onto a chair while he makes the dreaded phone call to the police. Emil tries to rehearse the words he will say to Caitlin. He does not make it past her name, however, barely comforted by Ben's presence, Emil shoots a text to his son.

Are you alright?

Junior responds in less than thirty seconds, *I'm fine, dad. What's up?*

Satisfied that Junior is safe, Emil decides against calling his school. Junior does not yet need to be plunged into the chaos, that is now the case of his missing sister. Ben and Emil are joined by Yolanda, Ben's older sister. The woman busies herself with making coffee, having brought over a pie.

Emil is unable to look at food, his stomach twisted in a permanent state of discomfort. In less than ten minutes, Emil's little safe and quiet bubble is transformed into a loud house with men and women in uniforms walking the length of the place. Units are on the scene, holding their radios and talking to each other discreetly as they scribble words on their small clipboards. Emil, mute, watches the scene. The sight of the officers brings back memories that were long buried in Emil's heart and the same feeling of helplessness returns. The feeling is overwhelming enough to cause tears to stubbornly roll down his face. Ben sits by his side, responding to the questions that the officers are asking.

Emil can hear an officer broadcasting over radio loudly "Twelve years old. White female, blonde, wearing a school uniform: a white blouse with a checkered skirt, goes by the name Paola. Additionally, she is not taking any medication and has no previous absconder reports. Start a detective and supervisor to our location."

Next to him, Ben cradles the telephone, calling Caitlin's office. Every time Emil tried to call, his voice failed him and cracked. He can't imagine her reaction. A voice in his head keeps yelling loudly at him, what she will scream, "How could you have let this happen?! Where is my baby! This is all your fault!" She will be right, he doesn't' have any answers. He doesn't know anything, Emil believes the voice wholeheartedly. It is his duty as a father to keep his kids safe. He has failed Paola. He has failed Caitlin.

"I should have followed her into the backyard," Emil says quietly to Ben. Ben shakes his head vigorously.

"No, Emil. You should not have because your daughter was reasonably safe within her own father's compound. Don't beat yourself up," Ben says softly before walking away quickly to inform Caitlin's employer on the phone.

"I should have followed her into the backyard," Emil repeats quietly to himself. Yolanda reaches out and places a wrinkled hand on Emil's. The woman had never been one for much talk but the gesture screams what her lips have not said. Do not do that. Do not do that.

There is the loud sound of cars arriving on the scene, but Emil's mind is distant. He rises from the chair he was sitting on and makes his way back to the backyard where some officers are, searching for leads and track marks. The officers are busy discussing among themselves but when Emil appears, their conversation dies instantly.

"What do we have?" A loud voice says. The men all turn in the direction of the voice. Flanked by two officers on both sides is a baldheaded man wearing sunglasses and casual clothes. He walks with the confident air of a superior. The officer in charge, Officer Sanchez, steps forward, nodding a greeting.

"We have a young girl missing. Five-five, slim and wearing school clothing," He reports and the man nods, taking in the entire scene in Emil's backyard. When his head turns towards Emil, his mouth opens slightly as he takes his sunglasses off. The world tilts on its axis as Emil recognizes the face of the old man. His hands suddenly turn sweaty as old memories and wounds resurface. What cruel game is fate playing? Of all the people who could be in charge, it's him. It all leaves a bad taste in Emil's mouth. The man steps forward, his mouth moving as the words come out.

"I'm Detective Me--"

"I know who you are, you have to find my little girl," Emil says harshly at the old man. The man appears taken aback by the venom in Emil's tone, but Emil could care less.

"Please, you owe me." He adds roughly. Detective Mesa stares at Emil, unblinking. Suddenly, a light bulb goes off in Detective Mesa's eyes, and his face, filled with remembrance, turns apologetic.

"Son, how are you? I looked for you for many years," Detective Mesa says, inching closer but Emil takes several steps back, his Adam's apple bobbing up and down.

"It doesn't matter." He says coldly, unable to meet the eye of the detective. "Just help me find my daughter." The other men watch in silence as Detective Mesa appears sober while Emil's face grows harder and harder with each passing second. The sound of someone crying filters into the backyard and Emil moves quickly, eager to get away from the Detective. The anguished cry could only be coming from one person.

Emil steps into the kitchen to see a red-faced Caitlin. Her mascara streaks down the sides of her eyes as she reaches for her husband amidst a choked sob.

"Where is my daughter, Emil? Where is my baby?" Caitlin weeps against his chest. Emil struggles to remain composed especially with all the officers staring at him. He holds her tight and lets her weep. He's going to have to remain strong for both of them, she needs to grieve.

It is when Emil disappears into the house that Detective Mesa can finally breathe easily, though his thoughts are scrambled within his head. The look on Emil's face that day in court haunted him for a long time and seeing him today simply brings back those haunting memories he tried so hard to forget. An image of a young Emil sleeping on a bench with his sister returns to mind and Detective Mesa squeezes his eyes shut, sad. On one hand, a part of him feels relieved to see how Emil turned out. From the looks of things, he seems to be stable with a wife and kids. On the other hand, another part of him is concerned about Emil's sanity and stability, especially where Emil's missing daughter is concerned. If anyone deserves to be happy and stable, it's Emil. He remembers Emil being flanked by a little girl and he wonders where his sister is. A resolution forms within Detective Mesa. Emil's daughter must be found. Detective Mesa whistles loudly.

"Sanchez, did you call K9?"

Officer Sanchez inches closer to him, "yes, they just arrived." Nodding, Mesa reaches into his pocket and pulls out a pack of cigarette. Pulling a cigarette out, he pulls out a lighter from his jeans and lights the cigarette.

"Man, I thought you quit!" says officer Sanchez

Mesa huffs as he puffs out a huge ring of smoke. "I wish!"

"Here, try some sunflower seeds, Sanchez offers. It helps me calm my nerves and helps me to focus." Mesa stares at the bag thoughtfully and pounders, smoking around the crime scene certainly isn't helpful, even though it seems to be the only thing that eases the tension in his spine these days. Sighing, he relents and puts out the cigarette. Detective Mesa takes the seeds and begins to chew them.

Emil is nowhere to be seen as Detective Mesa rallies the K9 team. The dog is released , and with Detective Mesa trailing behind them, they begin the search. The dog begins sniffing and slowly leads them towards Ben's yard. Unlike Emil's, it is organized: void of any toys, with a shed in the back. Ben, who was already back inside his house with Yolanda, walks out as the troop of officers descend into his backyard. The dog barks loudly at Ben's locked shed.

"Is everything okay, officers?" Ben asks as he approaches them.

"Sir, can you open your shed?" One of the K9 handlers asks.

"Sure thing," Ben nods as he reaches into his pocket for a bunch of keys. Mesa watches carefully as he opens it and with a smile, gestures for them to go in. Detective Mesa walks inside, chewing the sunflower seeds thoughtfully. The only thing that's inside the shed is a ride-along lawn mower. Confused, Detective Mesa spits his sunflower seeds involuntarily onto the wooden floors.

"Is that dog crazy or what are we doing?" Detective Mesa says with a raised voice. The K9 handler blushes, his face turning red.

"Sorry, Sir. He is a young track dog but a good tracker. I do not understand. He is probably picking up another track," he explains. Detective Mesa turns to Ben, shaking his head. He says "I'm sorry, sir. You know animals are not the brightest." Ben, with his hands in his pockets, simply nods, and says "No problem, I understand." Detective Mesa looks at the sunflower seeds he spat onto the ground, wincing, he points at them, "Sir, I will come back and clean those seeds."

"Ahh, don't worry about that, Officer. The main priority is finding the young woman," Ben states firmly, as he nods towards Emil's house in sympathy.

The Detective agreeably nods, "Absolutely, do you mind writing a statement for me? Of everything you saw and how you became involved?" One of the officers hands the Detective a clipboard, which he passes over to a willing Ben. Ben nods as he begins to scribble furiously while the officers wait. When Ben is done, the Detective takes the clipboard and says

"Here is my business card, call if you remember anything else and once again, thank you for your help."

"No problem, officer." Ben replies

The K9 teams lead the dog back out onto the streets as he keeps trying to track Paola's scent. The K9 handler yells, "detective we have a scent." The other officers hearing this, storm out of Ben's yard. After a few fruitless hours, the dog seems to have lose the track and is no longer picking anything up. Detective Mesa watches the failed attempts by K9, as he chews the seeds fast and intense.

"Detective, there's nothing here," Officer Sanchez says, looking bored. Detective Mesa wishes he could send his fist into the man's bored face. This is a life we're talking about here! An entire family, he wants to yell as he instead irritated grits his teeth.

"Take them into the backyard one last time he commands through gritted teeth. The girl's scent surely couldn't have disappeared into thin air," losing his patience, he barks loudly and the officer quickly follows orders and leads the team back into Emil's backyard.

Detective Mesa stands in front of the house, examining it, as he racks his brain for possible theories. He thinks to himself, the girl had been looking for cat and in less than one minute, she's nowhere to be found. "It was either a neatly done job with someone who had a car or she's still here somewhere," He murmurs to himself. He glances at the windows of Emil's house, he is startled to find a face staring back at him: squinting, he realizes that it's the cold face of Emil. Detective Mesa's tense posture eases as pity washes over him for Emil. Emil's eyes are vacant, and a chill runs down Detective Mesa's spine. It's the same look he had in his eyes that night. Detective Mesa raises a hand and waves towards Emil, to elicit a reaction out of him, but Emil does not blink. He stares at him, distant.

"We will find her," Detective Mesa mouths to Emil. Even though he cannot hear him, he hopes Emil can see the sincerity in his eyes but whether or not he does, Detective Mesa makes the promise again.

"I will find Paola."

Nothing can lift off the heavy sadness in Detective Mesa's chest but when he walks into the bar that evening, his chest feels relatively lighter, knowing that the liquor he's about to drink will help push the weight downwards. The bar buzzes with activity but Detective Mesa's sole attention is on the bartender serving drinks.

"My usual. Three shots."

"Whoa. Rough day?" The young bartender asks in surprise. Riley is dressed formally tonight, her hair packed in a ponytail. Tony must be in town; he thinks to himself.

"The worst," Detective Mesa mumbles as he balances on a stool, sighing deeply. He likes to be prepared for everything and anything but seeing Emil shook him to his core. The man's vacant eyes appear in his mind again and he rubs his forehead, displeased with his throbbing head.

"Do you have a headache?" Riley asks as she places a shot in front of him. "I've got some aspirin in the back if you'd like."

"Pour the drink, sweetheart. Nothing this can't cure," he says in a mock toast before pouring it down his throat. Riley watches him, concerned. The big hulk of a man looks sad, and she wishes she could help.

"Want to talk about it?" Riley asks softly as she takes other drink orders, her eyes on Detective Mesa. He shakes his head as he gestures for another drink and says "Not yet. Pour me some more."

"I sincerely hope you're not planning on driving yourself, Detective. If so, I'll be the one to report you myself," Riley says firmly and brings a smile to his face.

When Riley first came into town and started working as a bartender, it was hard to get her to talk or even show any emotion whatsoever. Now, she hovers over most of her customers like a mother hawk and they in turn look out for her too. For Mesa, Riley is like the daughter he never had. His stupid therapist had spoken about it once and surprisingly, he never disagreed. Instead, he acknowledged it. Yes, he has always wanted a daughter, but his ex-wife was not big on kids, and she left him before he could even say, I like kids, let us have some.

As he starts in on his second round, he says to her "Don't worry. I'll call a cab and come pick up the car in the morning." The drinks are not having the effect he hoped for, the weight in his chest simply gets heavier. He places his head in his hands for a few minutes as he tries to block out the noise in the bar, but it does not work. When he looks up, Riley is staring down at him.

"How about some comfort food? That works for me all the time when I'm sad."

"And what exactly will be in this comfort food?"

Riley shrugs. "For you, a little bit of everything. chicken, pasta, shrimp. Heck, I'll even throw in some coleslaw if you want." Detective Mesa chuckles, "then bring it on love." Without wasting time, Riley heads into the kitchen behind the bar. Bits and pieces of the conversation he had years ago with Nancy and Ricks come back to his mind. We did not do our best. **I did not do my best,** he thinks. The words of his therapist echo simultaneously, *"you did your legal best, Mesa, and that is okay."*

"Hello there, handsome."

A middle-aged woman is staring at Detective Mesa in a sultry manner. Her blonde hair has streaks of grey, she is in a dress that for Mesa, he considers too tight. Though he has not been with a woman in years, the thought of this woman with cakey makeup is not appealing. He gives her a small nod and simply turns back to face an approaching Riley.

"You're the quiet type, uh?" The woman chuckles as she settles on the stool beside him. Mesa shrugs as Riley places a plate of delicious-smelling food.

"Dig in!" Riley chirps, and glances at the woman who orders a drink. Detective Mesa can feel the woman's stare boring into his skin, demanding his attention but he refuses to oblige her.

Persistently "I see you're a food lover. What's your favorite meal?" she asks sweetly but Detective Mesa pretends not to hear her. The woman's face soon turns red from embarrassment and when Riley hands her a drink, she hisses and mutters a curse as she leaves Detective Mesa's side.

"You could have at least responded." Riley says.

Detective Mesa shakes his head. "That would have encouraged her, don't you think?

Riley gives up and sighs "ok, let's talk about you, Mister Brooding Detective. What's got your knickers all up in a twist?" Mesa sighs, he picks at his teeth with his finger before Riley, irritated, smacks his hands away.

"I saw someone today. Someone from my past and seeing him...seeing him was rather unexpected, and yet relieving too but also sad. It was a cluster of emotions for me. I felt like I failed him in the past and I wanted to tell him that. How I tried to look for him and help him out and all."

"So why didn't you tell him all of that?"

"He didn't want to hear it and I could scarcely blame him." Detective Mesa pokes at the chicken with while Riley stares at him thoughtfully.

"Do you have a son, Mesa? Is that what this is about?"

Detective Mesa snorts. "Really, Riley? How would you even think that? What did I say to give you that impression?"

Riley shrugs with a smile. "You sounded weird, I guess, and all the phrases you were using. I figured I'd give it a try. I guess the guys were right."

"Right about what?"

"They were talking about how you always treat crime victims so kindly and compassionately. I don't know who this person is but I'm sure he's someone you're not related to, but in your mind, you've probably concluded you owe him." Detective Mesa stops chewing, seeing Riley in a new light. The mischievous woman winks and Detective Mesa chuckles in return.

"You don't even know what happened" he retorts.

"I don't need to, but here's what I do know: you are a good person. You have always been, and you will do the right thing regardless. My advice? Don't be so hard on yourself, Detective, and allow yourself to breathe."

CHAPTER 8

There's never anything good about mornings and Detective Mesa is a strong advocate for that. His cup of black coffee lies on the table by his tall stack of documents. The night had been rather long for Detective Mesa. Seeing Emil again meant his night, and possibly more nights were disturbed. Unable to sleep, he kept tossing and turning. When he finally managed to fall asleep, his dreams were punctuated with images of crying and injured Emil. The last therapist told him that he felt so deeply for Emil simply because he related with him, since he too had not had the best of childhoods. He told her to go to hell even though he knew she was right. She was right but no one has to know about his childhood. He was past that now....mostly.

The station hums with activity as officers move around, yelling commands and requests. Seated within his small office, his head buzzing slightly, as a dull headache throb. He groans, as he reaches for the cup of coffee, he takes a long gulp, hardly tasting the lukewarm coffee. On his desk are pictures of Emil's house and pictures of Paola. He spent the previous night scouring over the case file, trying to see what they had missed. They interviewed all the neighbors, and no one saw anything. No one heard anything. Detective Mesa groans as he swirls the cup around. Come on, Paola. Let me find you.

"Anything yet?" A voice interrupts his thoughts. Detective Mesa looks up and into Detective River's curious blue eyes. He shakes his head, sighing loudly as he rubs his eyes.

"No, man. I do not understand how it could happen. She is now the third little girl missing in the past five years. No connection, no M.O or any similarities," Detective Mesa says dejectedly as he leans back into his chair with a deep sigh. Detective Rivers stands with arms akimbo in front of Detective Mesa. Unlike him, Rivers is younger and calmer in handling matters than Mesa. The buzzing sound of a telephone fills the room. When Mesa does not reach for it, Rivers reaches for the phone.

"Detective's office. Detective Rivers, can I help you? Oh okay. We are on the way." When Detective Rivers puts the phone down, he glances at Mesa with a grim look.

"What?" Mesa asks.

Detective Rivers gestures towards the door. "Make that number four."

Detective Mesa swears loudly as he rises immediately, joining Rivers they head outside. The car is ready, and the detectives jump inside. Mesa settles in the passenger seat, a place unknown to him, however, he is not able to drive due to his current turmoil.

"Where are we headed?" Mesa asks Rivers who is busy fixing his seatbelt in the Driver's seat.

"The river's edge by the trail, they found a body" says Rivers Grimly. Mesa remains quiet as the car zooms off downs the street. His mind replays all the memories with Emil and panic sets in. If there is a fourth number, then certainly, Emil may not recover his daughter alive. The realization hits Mesa in the gut and he finds himself quiet, unable to engage.

When they arrive on the scene, Detective Mesa grudgingly gets out. The crime scene is as a dark wooded area next to a river, close to an overpass, and close to railroad tracks. The cold body of an elderly woman lies on the dirty ground with stab wounds all over her chest. Detective Mesa groans as he inspects the body. The location where she was found, is not a usual dump site for bodies. The woman has a footprint on her face, with a single piece of sunflower seed shell where the footprint was marked, and several other pieces near the body.

"Detective, they just found a car idling in the High River community in the area where the kidnappings are occurring, approximately 200 yards from here" an officer Detective Mesa cannot recognize says aloud. Detective Rivers turns to face him while Mesa scoots down, trying to get a closer look at the woman's wounds.

Rivers says sternly, a hint of frustration in his voice: "Copy, run the tags, and determine who owns it, let's see if we can ID the registered owner and compare the driver's license info to the decedent, get me a full listing. In addition, this woman doesn't fit the kidnapper's modus operandus. Find out who she was and if anyone lives with her. Officer, I need that by yesterday!"

"Roger!"

Detective Mesa rises slowly, his inspection done. "He is fucking smarter than us, but we are getting close because he is getting sloppy," he says softly, looking down at the body. Detective Mesa's mind is trying to put the pieces together.

Detective Rivers scoots down to examine the body. He shakes his head as he assesses the body. "Closer, huh? You call this getting closer?" how? if this body doesn't match the kidnappers' M.O.

Detective Mesa looks at Rivers with a deep and dark look and explains, look at her neck, she has obvious sings of strangulation, like the kidnapped/murdered victims. However, this time, the perpetrator also stabbed her and kicked her in the face. He was extremely angry, and he over killed her during his rage. Furthermore, all the murders are within the 5 mile radius of High River community, he is extremely comfortable in this area.

Suddenly mesa stops his explanation, he trails off as he thinks to himself, wait... Paola hasn't been found yet; the other bodies were all found. Could we have a second murderer in our hands? Where are you princes, talk to me. Mesa comes back to the moment, he looks at Rivers, who is staring at him in confusion waiting for him to finish what he was saying.

Mesa continues "With every scene we have found that the victims have had the footprint, same size and brand, on their faces. We can find more clues to understand the perpetrator more."

"That's if it's one person who's doing these crimes," Detective Rivers interjects, not convinced there is only one perpetrator.

Detective Mesa sighs frustrated, his hands itching for a cigarette. Where is that damn officer with the sunflower seeds when you need him, he thinks to himself.

Mesa continues "Either way, there's bound to be a clue around here. Look at those stab wounds, retrieving DNA from them will certainly be helpful."

Detective Rivers places his hand under his chin, looking thoughtfully. A shrill ringtone pierces the air and Detective Rivers reaches for his cellphone tucked somewhere in his jacket.

"Detective Rivers."

A low and nervous voice says; "Hey, you better get to Fifth & Park Street we have another body."

Detective Rivers whistles, and says, "Mesa, we have another one"

Both detectives rapidly enter their cruiser with Mesa as the driver and leave the scene.

"What the hell is going on?" Detective Mesa murmurs under his breath as he races down the busy streets, the siren buzzing loudly on the car. Beside him, Detective Rivers clutches his seatbelt tightly.

"You might want to slow down there, Mesa. Whether we speed down there or not, the crime has been committed."

Detective Mesa glances at him through the side of his eyes as he slowly presses the brake. He did not realize that he was speeding. "Sorry," he apologizes sheepishly as Detective Rivers gives him a small smile.

For the rest of the ride, Detective Mesa's head works like clockwork. The pieces of the case are not adding up yet. Paola, the old woman by the river and a fifth body? Is this a serial killer or a maniac killing randomly on the loose? He glances at Rivers from the corner of his eye and his counterpart does not appear as concerned. Rivers has always been a calm man, the opposite of Mesa's fiery personality. They work well together. He is the only one who understands his moods well enough to know that a cranky Mesa simply means he either has not gotten coffee, or spent most of the night working. Rivers also had an uncanny ability for dates. He remembered dates Mesa did not remember like the day he got divorced. The day Detective Mesa was promoted. It was the little things like that, that made him trust Rivers more than anyone.

The GPS leads them to a tall, abandoned house, three streets away from Emil's house. Cruisers are parked by the lawn, and the paramedics have already arrived, ready to pick up the body. As they exit the car, Detective Mesa grabs his notebook hurriedly as Rivers steps in his way looking fidgety.

"What?"

"Partner, you should sit this one out. I got it, man," he says softly, surprising Detective Mesa. The only time Rivers uttered those words was years back on another child assault case like Emil's. Detective Mesa's face turns red with annoyance. Rivers only pulls shit like this when he thinks he is not composed enough to handle a situation, or he wants to protect his old partner.

"What the fuck are you talking about? We are in this together and when we nail this motherfucker, I'll retire, or you aren't going nowhere." River's eyes widen at his statement. Mesa has not spoken about retirement, since Emil's case; even though Rivers has mentioned his to plans retire many times.

Detective Mesa rolls his eyes "You're trying to make me let you go without me, aren't you? say whatever you want, Rivers. We nail him together, we retire together, or we stay, that is the choice I'm laying down for you. You can either take it or leave it."

River's sigh, crossing his arms; "Look, I'm just trying to look out for you. Do not think I haven't noticed the sour mood you have been in for most of the day. Even a while ago, I saw everything at that young man's house, and he reminds me of a certain---"

"Don't you finish that fucking statement, Rivers, You've noticed it, yes. Does that now make me too incompetent to do my job?" Mesa barks at him.

As Rivers tries to wrap his head around Mesa's statement, the paramedics come out of the house, pulling a stretcher along with them. There is a body covered with a blanket and the two detectives watch until the paramedics are inches away from them.

"What the fuck? Who is that?" Detective Mesa inches closer to lift the blanket. The ghastly sight causes him to stagger backward. Rivers grabs him just in time as he leans back on the car. His face is pale as he covers his mouth, tears filling his eyes. Detective Rivers risks a peek at the body, and he inhales sharply upon the sight.

"Damn," he says softly and gestures for the paramedics to leave. They waste no time loading the ambulance with the body. Meanwhile, Mesa reeling in anger, kicks the open door of the nearest cruiser.

"Man, what the fuck!" The officer inside the cruiser yells loudly. He steps out to push Mesa, cutting in Detective Rivers pointing his finger yells loudly, "Get the fuck back and sit in your fucking car as he pushes the officer back."

The officer raises his hands in surrender and slowly inches back into his car. Rivers runs a hand through his hair as he tries to regain composure. He glances at an exhausted Mesa.

"Bro, what the hell are you doing? Get yourself together!"

"Mesa says with a choked voice as if he is struggling with his emotions, "I am done. We are humans. Why are we killing each other in this manner? Who could do that to a child? She was a child."

"Mesa, I understand you brother, but you need to disassociate your emotions!" Rivers says, clapping his hands together, to shock Mesa back into the moment. Mesa grits his teeth in frustration. Too much is happening at the same time. His brain feels like it is tilting on its axis. He knows he has to get it together but it's all colliding the past, the present, he is failing again.

"Let's get back on the horse, or people will never have closure. Do you hear me?" Rivers' voice is loud and commanding, a part of him that people rarely see. Mesa sighs as he rubs his face, tired. Rivers is right. He needs to get his shit together.

"I'm sorry man." Mesa says in surrender.

"I don't need your apology. Let us go in there and do our damn job. That's what we are here to do." Trailing behind him, Mesa follows quietly, too exhausted to do or say anything else. When it is time to ask questions, he lets Rivers do it all.

*************Emil running in the streets********

There is a cloak of heaviness Emil that he can't shake off.

It does not matter how many runs or showers he takes. It simply refuses to leave, and Emil has no willpower to fight it. The only thing keeping him sane is his running every morning. Emil runs like his life depends on it. Lately, the neighbors have been pausing to stare. News of Paola's disappearance spread like wildfire. Emil knows, without anyone telling him, that his neighbors now lock their doors early and they refuse to let their kids play outside anymore either. Their street used to be a symphony of voices, especially in the afternoon on Saturdays but now, it is absolutely deserted, no child in sight.

Emil runs faster and faster, pushing himself to do more but his muscles refuse. This is the best we can do, they seem to say. There is no outrunning your pain or sadness. This is as far as we can take you. His nights have become more disturbed and the dreams more cryptic. They always ends up one way - with Emil hearing the sound of a crying Paola coming from a locked dark room and whenever he opens the door, Paola's lifeless body stares back at him. Caitlin is not having any luck either, her sleep gone. Every night, she sits by the window, peering out, waiting for Paola. Sometimes, he will join her and other times, he will sit in the backyard, weeping horridly. Thankfully, Ben always catches him at the right time, helping him back up. It has been a while, feels like forever since Paola went missing and Emil is in dire need of answers. He needs his daughter back home.

Pausing to catch his breath, Emil realizes he forgot Junior at home. His son had asked to come along with him for his run, but he barely remembers anything these days. Junior is equally having a horrid time especially concentrating in school. Emil tries as much as he can to keep the house in shape, making meals for Jr. whenever he returns from school but he knows it is not enough. It is not how Caitlin would do it. Emil glances at the watch on his hand as he pants, aching for water. He exhales heavily, hoping for some good news today, before running again. This time, he runs in the opposite direction.

Every little girl looks like Paola. It is so terrible that Emil worries he might kidnap somebody's daughter but deep down, he knows he can't. No girl is like his girl, Paola. He considers calling up his therapist from before. She was the one who made him into the soft man he is today. Slowly ridding him of the trauma of his childhood. The back of his head throbs with dull pain, a reminder that he has not eaten in nineteen hours. As he runs, his phone vibrates against his pocket. He wants to ignore it, but the persistent ringing causes him to pick up, thinking it might be the police. He is surprised that it isn't.

"Emil" says the voice as he says "Sofia" simultaneously.

Though her voice is different and more mature, his sister's old voice threatens to bring back memories long forgotten. After their parents were gone, the siblings promised to live different lives separate from one another.

"We both need to heal, being together reminds us of too much" Sofia said to him years ago on her eighteenth birthday with a duffel bag packed, and a plane ticket to Los Angeles.

He did not stop her, he couldn't even if he tried because she was right. They both needed to heal since every time he looked at her, Sofia reminded of their mother.

"I heard the news, t's a terrible thing to happen to anyone. How are you fairing?" She asks quietly and Emil tries to speak, swallowing the bulge in his throat.

"Not well." His voice comes out croaky as his emotions rise to the surface. Hiding things from Sofia has always been difficult.

"I'm so sorry. If you need anything...." Sofia lets the invitation hang in the air, not saying any more.

"I will...I hope you're doing fine as well," He asks tentatively, aware of their existing rule of not asking about each other's lives.

"I'm well, Emil. I am well. I have to go now. Take care, okay?" Sofia responds.

"I will. And you too," says Emil as the call ends.

When the call ends, Emil sighs, exhaling a shaky breath. The last time he heard from Sofia was five years ago. Suddenly, he is there in the room, Sofia crying on the other side of the door, Emil shakes the memory away. He does the only thing he knows how to. He runs and he keeps running with the wind rushing past his ears. Emil feels nothing but the welcoming ache of his body as he runs, pressing on with the great force and might to numb everything else. However, every journey must come to an end and soon, Emil is running down the familiar path to his house. Tired, he slows down, panting heavily.

The familiar markings along his street make his heart squeeze with pain. Memories of Paola playing along the street, dancing ahead of him with flowers in her hair haunt him. The wind carries her voice and her smell so that with every step he takes, his heart crushes even more and more. The cloak he had on returns, it hangs even more heavily around his shoulders. There is a car parked along the street and Emil notices it, as he walks up the path leading to his house.

The lawn overgrown with weeds and Emil has no desire to cut it. They reflect the state of his mind and the state of his heart. Emil climbs up the stairs with the agility of a sixty-year-old man, dreading entering his house. When he does, heaviness descends on his head leaving him tired, beaten, and devitalized. He approaches the board by the window and scribbles the license plate across it, routines must remain.

****

"Come on, man. Do we have to do this?" asks Mesa.

Rivers glances from the corners of his eyes at a reluctant Mesa. Since their last visit to Emil's place, his partner has not been the same; there are visible dark circles underneath his eyes and even his pallor is different. Something has switched within him, and Rivers does not like it. He does not like that Mesa has become a shadow of himself. Day after day, he pores over the case file like a dog looking for a bone, frustration etched into his forehead. Rivers sighs, feeling equally terrible, "you know we have to, a couple of questions arose at the station and Emil is the only one who can answer them."

"You could go there alone," Mesa murmurs but Rivers does not respond, knowing full well that Mesa would have bugged him if he refused to let him come along. Instead, he focuses on the soft country music playing in the background from the car radio. He thinks to himself, how he cannot wait to retire. His grandkids are expecting him, and he cannot wait to see them. He also cannot wait to stop driving a cruiser. It's been nearly forty years. Rivers comes back to the moment, and he asks Mesa "want to come by for dinner? My wife will make your favorite, I promise." Mesa only grunts, not giving a yes or a no. Sighing Rivers shakes his head, he turns into Emil's street. Nothing can separate Mesa from the love of his case. Not even tasty food.

When Rivers pulls over in front of Emil's house, his partner's face becomes even sadder. His sadness is so palpable that Rivers places his hand on his arm.

"You've got this, Mesa. I will be right there with you. You've got this."

Mesa nods as they both step out. An overgrown lawn greets the men as they lock the cruiser and make their way up to Emil's house. Rivers catches a glimpse of Emil in the window, and he sighs. As expected, the man is also a shadow of himself. Rivers exhales. The interrogation is either going to end well or terribly. He moves ahead of Mesa and knocks, standing in front as though to protect his partner from Emil. When the man opens, Rivers releases the breath he had been unconsciously holding and says "Hello, sir."

"Detectives," Emil murmurs, leaving the door ajar and walks back in. The two Detectives make their way into the house. The loss of their daughter hangs in the air, filling the air and everything in the house with a compressing sorrow.

"Please, tell me you found my daughter," Emil's voice shakes and Rivers feels his throat close, he suddenly becomes unable to speak. It is Mesa who comes to his rescue, stepping forward, "not yet Emil. We have some questions for you." There's an unidentifiable emotion across Emil's face as he stares at the two Detectives.

"You have questions for me" He repeats with a haunting look. In a split second, his face transforms and he glares at the detectives.

"FOR ME? Why aren't you looking for my daughter?" he yells. Startled, Mesa steps backward, his mouth flapping as he tries to explain but Emil would not let him.

"OH, let me guess. It is just another file on your desk, or wait, you must make a fucking perfect case before you waste your time?" He yells again, his voice reverberating off the walls. Rivers sighs as he assesses the young distraught father. He is on the brink of a mental breakdown and their presence certainly isn't helping matters. It never does unless it is good news.

As Mesa tries to find the right words to say, Emil's wife, Caitlin, steps into the living room. Her eyes are red and heavy, worse than Emil's. Her lithe movements catch Emil's attention and his face changes instantly to a mild and soft one. Staring at the two detectives, she seems to get what is happening, and her eyes slowly turn glassy.

"Emil, please, she pleads, our daughter is still missing. Please" she blubbers as she tries to stifle the sobs. Emil inches closer to her, he pulls her into a warm hug. There's unmistakable pain in his eyes. "I'm sorry. I am sorry, baby," He mumbles, running a hand through her hair. His Adam's apple bobs up and down as he closes his eyes.

"I can't do this. She is just a baby," Emil murmurs over his wife's head at the detectives. The sight of the weeping parents is too emotional for Mesa, and he turns away, his throat tightening making it hard to speak.

"Sir, detective Rivers interjects, I can assure you that the police department is doing everything we can to find her." Rivers pauses briefly, he takes in the scene: the frantic parents, his distressed partner, Rivers realizes he is not going to get anywhere. He reluctantly decides for the time being he is going to leave things alone. "If there are no questions from you, we will leave now. We will keep you updated." Neither parent responds, tucked in their embrace, holding on to hope and each other. Rivers places his hand on Mesa's shoulders, and he notices his glassy eyes.

"Partner, let's go."

Mesa nods and with a final glance at the couple, the two detectives find their way out. When they step out onto the porch, Rivers inhales deeply, letting go of all the sadness that may have welled up within him. Mesa stays quiet, he knows his partner is struggling to keep his emotions at bay.

As they make their way to the cruiser, the sound of someone humming draws their attention. Standing on his property, merely a few meters away is the kind neighbor, Ben. He acknowledges the detectives with a nod, he abandons his bushes and makes his way towards the detectives.

"Hey, detectives, any news on the murder of my neighbor's little girl?" Ben asks.

"We don't have anything else to add sir." Rivers responds and with an afterthought he reaches into his pocket, "here is my card and if you see or hear anything please let me know, thank you."

"Sure will, detectives, and please find her. They haven't been the same since she left." Ben says.

"We are doing our best," Mesa answers and Ben nods, giving him a small smile. Eager to leave, Mesa continues to walk towards the cruiser quietly, Mesa and Rivers reach their cruiser, they settle in, neither utters a word, instead, they drive in silence, ruminating.

"Your honor, this is an outrage. That is a child!" Detective Mesa yells above the noise within the courtroom. Judge Kenny's face contorts in anger.

"Detective, take your seat and remain quiet or I'll hold you in contempt of court. Bailiff!" Detective Mesa stares at Judge Kenny with contempt, looking livid as he advances upon Judge Kenny.

"Contempt of court. Is that all you can do?" Detective Mesa sneers angered. Surprise is visibly written across Judge Kenny's face as well as the attorneys.

"Bailiff, remove the Detective from my courtroom and remand him for a day!" Judge Kenny yells as Detective Mesa keeps yelling, annoyed. Emil watches, terrified. What exactly is happening? US marshals walk to Detective Mesa

and grab him by the arms. It is a wild scene as the Detective resists violently as he tries to pull away. His veins are visibly strained across his forehead as he points at Attorney Ricks and yells, "Emil is a child, a child who, like everyone is told to place their trust in us, THE SYSTEM!" Detective Mesa continues to yell and point at her "You betrayed him for your career, your career! You want society to trust the law? Trust the police? It does not matter what the law is or how good the police investigations are, because at the end of the day it's about wins for the prosecutors. You dismiss charges, put children on the stand because you do not want to 'loose,' you selfish bitch!" you don't care about the citizens, you only care about your stats. The Marshalls hold him in a tight grip, trying to haul him out. Attorney Ricks does not appear fazed. She stares back blankly at him.

"There is always another time, bro," One of the Marshalls, whispers against Detective Mesa's face hurriedly.

"Don't lose your job. Detective Mesa quiets down, a stony look on his face. As he passes Emil, Detective Mesa gives him a sad apologetic look.

"I'm sorry, Emil

"Should I drop you at home?" Rivers asks bringing Mesa out of his past memory trance.

Mesa shakes his pounding head. The thought of a quiet and dark home does not sound appealing to Mesa. He needs somewhere bright with lights where his dark thoughts can turn to mush. Bits and pieces of the words said in the courtroom that day haunt Mesa.

"Take me to the bar," Mesa sighs. "We're a minute away anyway."

"Are you sure you want to do that, Mesa?"

"Are you really sure you want to ask me questions, Rivers? Do you have a better place for me to go?" Mesa snaps. The thought to apologize instantly fills Mesa's mind but he pushes it back, that's what Rivers get for arguing with him.

"I think what you need is a really good meal and a long nap. You look like you have not been getting enough rest," Rivers says quietly.

"The only way I'll get any rest is if you drive me to that bar, Rivers. That is the only way I'll be getting any sleep tonight," Mesa says with less anger in his voice.

Rivers does not respond but his tight fists around the steering wheel say it all. Unfortunately, for Rivers, there is nothing else he can do to stop him. When Rivers pulls up in front of the bar, he gives Mesa a pointed look.

"Take it easy, man. Okay?"

"Drive safe" is all Mesa says as he gets out of the car and does not spare him a backward glance.

As usual, the bar is crowded but Mesa does not care for the crowd. Riley is standing by the bar and the moment she sees Mesa, she grabs a big bottle of vodka, shaking her head as she eyes the weary man.

"You certainly had a rough week," Riley says before placing three glasses in front of him.

"You can only imagine kiddo." Mesa takes the three shots in less than ten seconds and gestures for more. The duo repeats the action several times until Mesa's muscles ease of their own accord and his vision becomes less stable.

"I needed that," he says quietly, staring at the bottles behind Riley's head. With a smirk on her face, Riley cocks her head to the side.

"I think we should take a break now; don't you think?" Riley asks softly but Mesa chuckles, trying to reach for the bottle.

"You and Rivers are probably related, thinking you can both tell me what I can or cannot do. Silly goose."

"I guess Rivers and I are just trying to look out for you. You should be thankful," Riley mutters, grudgingly pouring another shot for him: Mesa takes it, Riley starts to pour another, but Mesa already feeling the effects of his liquor courage, smirks and puts a finger out to halt her, as he reaches for his phone and dials. He looks at Riley and drawls I know what to do," he places the phone against his ears. He hushes Riley who simply smiles, amused by a tipsy Mesa, and starts to say "If that's your ex-wife, this should be rather interesting."

Mesa hushes Riley with his finger as he says "Attorney Ricks. Nice to hear your voice again" into the phone slightly slurred.

"Who's this?" says the irritated female voice on the end of the call.

"Oh, you've forgotten my voice so easily. That is a shame. I could have sworn that I my voice would haunt you," Mesa chuckles drunkenly.

"Is this some type of joke? To whom am I speaking?" Ricks snarls and Mesa leans back into his chair, pleased that he has triggered her.

"This is Detective Mesa. I believe you and I have worked on a couple of cases together before you became a big city hotshot."

"Oh." There's disappointment in her voice. "And to what do I owe this unexpected phone call in the middle of the night, detective?"

"Remember Emil? The boy you refused to get justice for, who was being sexually assaulted by his stepfather?"

"I've represented a lot of clients who were being sexually assaulted over the years, Detective. Is there something you would like to say?" Attorney Rick's cold voice echoes over the phone and Mesa chuckles.

"Of course, and each one of them ended with a detective being thrown out of the courtroom, right?" There is an exasperated huff from Attorney Ricks.

"I barely remember, detective. It was a long time ago. Do you have a point?"

"You're rather good at lying. That is a bad trait for an Attorney, isn't it?"

"I'm very busy, Detective. Kindly get to the point."

"I found him and guess what? Thanks to you and all your corrupt friends in high places, life has not been easy. In fact, his daughter just got kidnapped and he is sinking lower and lower into depression," Mesa spits bitterly. Attorney Ricks audibly inhales.

"And how's that my fault? His daughters kidnapping has nothing to do with me. I think you should place a call to your friends at the station to discuss why there's so much crime and a lack of safety despite all the money and equipment you're all given."

"Oh, no, kidnapping is not your concern. Your concern is making deals and getting ahead in your career despite breaking people's spirits and belief in the system. Making people believe that the only justice they can find is in blaming the police who are the scapegoats for your deals."

"Goodbye, Detective." Before Mesa can utter another word, the phone line goes dead. The urge to throw the phone across the room fills Mesa but instead, he slides it across the counter, watching it go, he utters "she's an absolute useless piece of shit."

Riley sighs, placing the now filled small glass before Mesa.

"Drink up, mister detective. It appears we're going to need something stronger tonight."

CHAPTER 9

(Nine months later)

There is a woodpecker by the window and Emil's eyes follow its every movement as it pecks against the wooden window frame. Asides from cats, Paola also likes birds. Emil wonders if his daughter can see birds where she is. Can she see the sky and the stars at night? A memory of Paola chasing after birds in the park returns to Emil and he chuckles to himself. She was adorable that year with her pigtails and her chubby baby face.

"They're not waiting, Daddy," She had pouted sorrowfully that day.

"You have to let them come to you, baby. Do not chase them. Open your hands and let them come to you," He had advised, and she followed it. Soon, birds were perching on her shoulders and arms, eating out of the feed-in her hand. Her eyes had gleamed with excitement, and she nearly screamed to prove it.

The woodpecker draws Emil's attention back to reality and he focuses on the bird. Perhaps Doctor Winston might have some feed so he can...

"You're not listening, Emil." Caitlin's voice is hard and cold. It has been that way for nearly weeks now. Emil smiles at Doctor Winston, apologetically.

"My apologies. I now find it hard to focus for a long time. What did I miss?" Caitlin gives an exhausted sigh which Emil ignores.

"Your wife just spoke about her issues regarding your daughter disappearance. What are your own issues? What are your thoughts?" Doctor Winston asks kindly, but Emil is distracted by the number of books on the shelf behind him.

"I have no thoughts, Doctor Winston. I am still hopeful about the return of my daughter. The police officers haven't found a body so that means Paola is somewhere out there, alive."

"Emil, our baby girl is gone," Caitlin's voice shakes as she pleads with her husband. "She's nowhere to be found, Emil."

"What kind of mother are you?" Emil snaps, turning to Caitlin. Surprised, her mouth falls open. In all their years together, Emil has never snapped.

"It's been just nine months, Caitlin. Have you no faith?"

Caitlin's voice breaks "the police found dead bodies days after our daughter's disappearance. I no longer feel the connection I had with my daughter, Emil. I can't feel her anymore," she cries out reaching for the box of tissues in front of her.

Redirecting the attention to what Emil said the doctor says "attacking each other is not the point Emil. We need to talk

110

about everything we are feeling so we can be prepared for whatever happens. For whatever discoveries the police make."

Sarcastically Emil says, "You mean we need to be prepared for when the police locate the dead body of our daughter."

Exasperated Caitlin says "Can't you see that we're being torn apart because of this? Is this what Paola would want, Emil?"

"Is this what Paola would have wanted, Caitlin? For us to go to therapy to learn how to forget her?" Emil's voice goes up a notch.

Doctor Winston interjects "Let's all calm down here for a moment, okay? Let's have a minute of silence. Everyone should go over the conversation in their heads and think carefully about the next few words they want to say, okay?" The silence is thick with tension as the couple muse over their words. Emil glances towards the window, returning his attention to the woodpecker but the bird is gone. Their loud voices must have startled the poor thing. Emil exhales noisily, drawing Doctor Winston's attention.

The doctor's face is blank, unreadable, and inscrutable, she makes direct eye contact with them, and continues "a quick reminder as to why we are here. We are here to verbalize all your emotions about Paola's disappearance. We want to see how that is affecting your relationship as a couple and how you can both move forward from that."

"The only way forward is finding Paola's body," Emil mutters and Caitlin scoffs in return.

"If you have something to say, Caitlin, please do. Let me know how badly I have hurt you and disappointed you. How much you blame me for what happened," Emil, retorts.

"I never said I blame you, Emil. You're---"

"I'm what, Caitlin? Please speak freely. Let it all out of your mind."

"Yes, Emil. I blame you, you are at fault for not watching our daughter well enough," Caitlin snaps.

"What?" Emil asks weakly.

"Yes, Emil, I blame you! There! You wanted me to say it and I have! I blame you for not being out there with her. I blame you for her going missing!" Caitlin yells and tears pool out of her eyes.

Emil's hands turn sweaty as he takes in the mother of his children. The words pierce into Emil's chest and twist his insides with a fierce intensity. Caitlin is busy dabbing her eyes with a tissue.

"And what do you have to say to that, Emil?" Doctor Winston asks. Emil cannot find a response as he feels abashed with shock and embarrassment.

"There's nothing more to be said, Doctor Winston," Emil announces quietly, rising to his feet.

"Mister Emil, hold on. You need to understand that how your wife feels---" Emil dashes out of the room before Doctor Winston can conclude her statement. There is a stunned look in Emil's eyes as he pauses outside the door, trying to gather his thoughts.

"Are you okay, sir?" Doctor Winston's secretary asks. He barely hears her question as he moves robotically. Blood pounds within his ears as he makes his way out of the building. The moment his feet hit the gravel, Emil takes off running.

It's the only thing he knows how to do.

It's already dark outside when Emil returns home, sweating profusely.

He ran so hard till he got lost, meandering through the streets, trying to find his way back home. When he finally retraced his steps, the hunger in his belly made him stop by a burger shop, Emil enjoyed a few minutes of silence, while he ate. Contemplating his life and the argument he had with Caitlin. One thing remained constant all through the day - Caitlin's voice in the back of his head.

Yes, Emil. I blame you, you are at fault for not watching our daughter well enough.

The pain is fresh in his chest every time he remembers her words. All his life, Emil has lived with the knowledge that his mother blamed him for ruining her marriage. Even though she defended him in the end, her inactions stuck.

She only wanted her marriage to work. Even Sofia secretly blamed him for their misfortunes. It was one of the reasons she left, never to return to stay connected. His life inadvertently affected hers and if it had never happened, she would have had a better life.

The words come back again, yes, Emil. I blame you, you are at fault for not watching our daughter well enough.

The sight of their porch causes his heart to constrict. How can he sleep in the same bed with a woman whose heart is bitter towards him? There are no words to comfort her and there are no words for him either. When he inserts his key into the door and makes his way in, he nearly stumbles over a stack of suitcases by the door. Emil glances around, wondering why there are so many suitcases, and he sees Caitlin sitting on the couch alone, her eyes on him.

"What's going on?"

"I'm leaving, Emil," Caitlin says as she rises to her feet, dressed in a grey tracksuit. Junior leans against the wall, watching his parents with sad eyes.

"I can't stay here in this house. Junior can't stay here either. We need a new place to start new and heal. We can no longer wait for you to see reason," Caitlin says quietly. The resolution in her eyes is visible but Emil refuses to accept it.

"Caitlin, look, we need to be together as a family. We need to be here for Paola." He moves closer in a bid to touch her arm, but Caitlin takes a step back, shaking her head

"We're leaving, Emil." Jr. Needs us! Jr. needs you; he needs to have the opportunity to continue to live past this horrible tragedy, but you don't see it, you don't see him anymore you don't see me. I wasn't asking you to give up hope or forget about our daughter, I was asking you to remember your son.

Emil's hand falls to his side in defeat, her words stinging him. There will be no convincing Caitlin. He glances at his son who remains quiet, concern in his eyes.

Caitlin starts softly "I'm sorry about what I said in therapy. It is not your fault. It never was. My mind just needed someone to blame but my heart knows it's a lie."

"It doesn't matter, Caitlin. Before you blamed me, I already blamed myself. Watching and protecting our kids is my responsibility and I failed," Emil shrugs defeated.

Caitlin stares at him, trying to plead with him through her eyes for him to understand what she is saying but Emil looks away.

"I found a house five streets away from here. It's by the brown Cathedral on Silverstone and Gordon Street. If you want to join us, you're welcome to," Caitlin says quietly. When Emil does not respond, Caitlin gestures to Junior who picks up his school bag and grabs a suitcase.

"I'll send a company by to get the rest of our stuff in the morning. I'm not sure I want to come back here." Emil nods, staring anywhere but at Caitlin.

Caitlin moves to stand in front of her husband. Emil refuses to make eye contact with her but he is surprised when Caitlin leans in and places a soft kiss against his cheek.

"Whenever you're ready, come home," she whispers against his cheek. Tears threaten Emil's eyes, but he remains mute as Caitlin and Junior make their way out.

You can still stop them! Go, Emil, a voice echoes in his head but he ignores it. The voice pesters Emil, refusing him peace, and the grieved man dashes outside just as Caitlin's car is driving away.

"Caitlin!" He yells, running down the porch but his wife does not stop. Her car glides smoothly across the ground and moves towards the horizon. Emil falls to his knees on his lawn, and he lets out a strangled cry.

"Hey! You, okay?" Ben calls from his porch. Emil shakes his head as silent tears stream down his face.

"I'm not okay, Ben. I'm not okay," Emil whispers, staring down the dark street. Caitlin's car is gone and can no longer be seen.

"My wife is gone," Emil says before breaking down into an ugly sob. It's a matter of seconds before Ben wraps his arms around him, squeezing him tightly. Emil wheezes in his arms, his body wracked with heavy sobs.

"Why don't you go after her, Emil? I'm sure you guys can always work things out whatever it is," Ben says weakly but Emil shakes his head.

"There's nothing to be resolved, Ben. I can't go to hide away somewhere. I need to be here. I need to remain here for my daughter," Emil whispers brokenly. When he glances at Ben's eyes, the emotion there is a pity. There's something else behind them that Emil can't identify.

"Emil, I think you----"

"No," Emil growls. "Don't say it."

"Listen, Emil, you----," Emil jerks out of Ben's arms, falling backward onto the lawn. Ben moves forward to help him but Emil crawls backward, away from him.

"Don't." Emil's eyes are hard and, in a flash, Ben watches him take off, running without sparing him a backward glance. Though tears fill his eyes and drip down his face, Emil runs with the wind, and he refuses to stop.

If he is going to remain the only one who believes in Paola's return, then so be it.

CHAPTER 10

(Three months later)

It's barely ten in the morning and Mesa is already tired. He gulps more coffee, trying to stay awake but his eyes are tired. Every cell within his being is tired. Mesa recites his shouldn't have list: he shouldn't have spent the night at the bar. He shouldn't have taken that many drinks. He shouldn't have danced with the woman with the red lips. He shouldn't have let her kiss him and drag her lips all over his body. He shouldn't have let her into his bed. Even though he woke up in the morning, tired and with the promise that he will not do it again, Mesa knows it's all a lie. By three p.m., when the fatigue and the sadness hit him again, he will find himself contemplating and rationalizing his way back to the bar, crawling if he must. It's the only thing that brings temporary relief.

Since Emil's wife left the house and Emil disappeared into thin air, life took an awkward turn for Mesa. He fell into a depression, and nothing seemed to be working. He tried finding pleasure in food, but it soon lost its taste. He turned to the gym but soon the endorphin high lost its pleasure. Hence, the dependable alcohol that never fails to numb him.

"I've told you what will work. I need to find the answer to this case. Only then will I be able to find my joy and peace back," Mesa has told the department psychologist, whom he is forced to see after his drinking has led to a litany of bad choices.

Eventually, Rivers managed to organize a small intervention that has made him reassess his life choices. Though he's not quite out of the woods: last night being a prime example, his strong determination to find Emil is his compass. Today just might be the day that happens.

His informant on the streets has informed him about a man sleeping near a grave who fits Emil's exact description. Parked outside the cemetery, Mesa waits outside, watching the sleeping man. His clothes are torn, and his feet are nearly black with an assortment of scrapes and wounds. Mesa is torn between hoping that the crazy man sleeping on the ground is Emil or is not Emil.

A sound pierces the air and Mesa, wincing, grabs the phone, eager to make the ringing stop, so it won't alert the man to his presence.

"What?" He asks gruffly.

"I sincerely hope that you're awake, Mesa," Rivers sighs. "It's nearly ten o'clock. You should be here."

"I'm awake. I'm on the road and I'm chasing a lead," Mesa replies.

"Oh. That's good," Rivers sounds surprised and Mesa resists the urge to smile. As annoying as Rivers could be, he is the only one who looks out for him. Mesa appreciates him more than anything.

"Yeah. I should be at work soon. Hopefully, in an hour," says Mesa

"I'll tell the Chief then. Be safe out there, okay? I'd ask you to grab a bite for me from Nialles Diner but I'm not exactly sure when you'll be back," Rivers speaks bigheartedly.

"You don't have to tell me twice, Buddy. I'll get your damn food" Mesa replies.

The call ends and when Mesa returns his gaze back to the cemetery, he nearly jumps out of his seat. The sleeping man is being chased by a security guard. Mesa watches in horror as the man, whose hair and beard are overgrown, turns out to be Emil. His heartbeat picks up as he watches Emil run out of the cemetery and further away.

Summoning up courage, Mesa steps out of his car, instead of following the running man, Mesa makes his way into the cemetery. Although cemeteries are spooky for him, he keeps moving, making his way towards the grave where Emil was lying. The cemetery guard nods in greeting, returning from his chase, his forehead furrowed in concentration, but Mesa doesn't respond. Mesa walks to the tomb and his heart nearly stops as he reads the tombstone. Emblazoned boldly across is Paola's name. It all makes sense now. Mesa rubs his face as the fatigue kicks in again. He could really use a drink. The guard is hanging around near another grave, picking something up. Mesa inches closer to him, calling out to him while showing the guard his badge. The guard nods as he rises slowly. He is shorter than Mesa and the only feature about him that's worth speaking about is his mousy brown hair.

"Hey, who was that? That was here earlier."

"I guess he's the father."

Detective Mesa nods his head as he glances away to look at Paola's grave. In one quick motion, he lunges and grabs him by the neck. Mesa holds him down and leans against him, a furious look on his face. Mesa yells into the guard's face "His daughter was never found. He lost everything! EVERYTHING! All he needs is a bit of fucking empathy! and all you, a fucking rental cop, can do is kick him while he is down. Listen you bitch, if I ever see you do such a thing again, I will put you in a hole so deep you won't be able to talk if you ever crawl out. Do we understand each other?" As he pushes him away with such force that the security guard lands on his back, terror on his face.

"Yes, sir. Yes, sir. I understand!" He replies in fright.

Mesa watches with regret as the guard runs from him, terrified.

He shouldn't have shouted. Mesa turns around to stare at the tomb again. Emil's wife did go ahead to organize a funeral then. Mesa sighs as he wipes his face.

"Listen, kiddo. I don't know where you are. I don't know how you're faring, but I promise you I will find you." Mesa pauses but all he gets in response is the wind's soft rustle. "Your Dad comes here every day to sleep by you and I

121

hope wherever you are, you're fighting. For him...and for me too." Mesa exhales as he keeps staring at the tomb, a brave face on but deep down, he wonders if he will truly ever find her.

CHAPTER 11

Emil recalls one of the last conversations he had with his wife before she left:

"That was a really good movie. Junior enjoyed it," Emil says lazily as he draws circles along his wife's back.

"I'm sorry, Emil, but I cannot do this anymore," Caitlin whispers as he holds her in a warm embrace. Emil pats her head gently.

"Just close your eyes, Caitlin. Just close your eyes. The meds should kick in soon."

"No, Emil. That's not what I mean. I cannot do THIS anymore." Scared, Emil pulls back to stare at his wife's eyes. She's not crying. That gives him, even more, to worry about.

"You want a divorce?" He whispers and Caitlin sits up, her eyes wide as she realizes his mistake.

"No, God, no. I can't imagine my life without you, especially not after everything we've been through," Caitlin says softly, touching his arm to convince him. Looking into her eyes, Emil is convinced. That's not what she meant.

"Then, what do you mean by 'this'?"

"She's gone, Emil. She's not coming back. She's never going to come back." The words are delivered so softly but they hit Emil with a crumbling weight.

"Never say that again, Caitlin." Emil's voice is cold as he inches away from her like she has a plague. Caitlin looks heartbroken at her husband's reaction, and she reaches to touch him, but he springs up from the bed.

"Never say that again, Caitlin! Our baby girl is out there somewhere, praying to come back home and her mother, the one person who should believe in her reappearance the most, has given up! Don't ever say that again, Caitlin. If you have given up, I haven't!"

"I had a dream. Paola was dead in it," Caitlin says in a monotone voice.

"Have another one where she's alive in it because she is."

The sun is high up in the sky and while Emil would ordinarily run, looking for shelter, his strength has deserted him. The pain is intense, Emil clutches his stomach, moving slowly as he trudges along the sidewalk. The last time he ate a decent meal was nearly forty-eight hours earlier. As he comes across people on the sidewalk, they inch away from him, scared of him. Every time this happens, Emil wants to tell them that they have nothing to be afraid of. What they have to be afraid of is out there in the great unknown, ready to claim them and their loved ones, however, he doesn't. There is an overflowing trash can nearby and Emil rushes towards it, ransacking the can, trying to find something in it. The sound of giggling children is what draws him out of his introspective state. That is when he sees it.

Though there is a metallic fence stopping strangers from entering, the school's field is wide and littered with children. Most of them are running around in different directions. Some are playing soccer. Some are dancing, others cheerleading. Some are not doing anything, and it is that group that catches his eye. Someone in the group in particular catches his eye. Almost immediately, the young boy turns in his direction and notices the weird man staring at him. Unlike what other kids would do, he runs towards him and places a finger through the metallic net, a sad expression on his face. Emil holds back tears as he touches his finger in return.

"Daddy, is that you? Please, talk to me, daddy!" Junior exclaims as he tries to touch his father further through the net but is unable to.

"Hi, son. I've missed you," Emil says, choking on a sob. "And your mother and..." He takes in a deep breath, trying to regulate his breathing but he fails miserably.

"Daddy, we miss you too. Please, come home," Junior begs. "Mom cries every day and goes to sleep calling you. Please, Dad."

Emil stares at his dirty feet, remembering his wife. Memories of her often come in bits and pieces. He remembers her the most whenever he walks into the cemetery and sees that old couple who come to visit their friends. Sometimes, he remembers her when he sees people walking down the streets, holding hands.

"She does?"

"Yes! She talks about you all the time and she doesn't even sleep so well without you." A smile begs to be let free on Emil's face but just as quickly as it appears, the smile is replaced with a frown.

"I can't, son. Your sister needs me. I have to look for her," Emil says softly, his eyes looking distant. "She needs..." He trails off, the sound of a loud bell interrupting him. Junior glances back, realizing that his classmates are all rushing back inside.

"Dad, you've got to ---"

"Junior! Please, come here!" The loud voice of one of his teachers rings out loudly. A pained look comes upon Junior's face. Mustering all the strength he can, Junior reaches for his father's fingers.

"Please, Dad. Just think about it and come home. We're staying at five, Gordon Street now, okay? Promise me please," He begs urgently but Emil can only shake his head, the tears have returned in full force.

"Junior! Please, come here now!" His teacher yells again. Junior sighs, looking disappointed.

"Love you, daddy," He mutters.

"Love you too, son."

Junior makes his way to his teacher, running towards her, and Emil watches, transfixed, with his hands on the net. When Junior reaches his teacher, he turns around to wave, and Emil spots the wet sheen of tears on his face. The sight breaks him even further as he waves in return, wishing he could hug him. As his son disappears into the school building, Emil lets out a painful groan as he doubles down in pain, crying.

This was not how things were supposed to go.

It has been days since Mesa found Emil and in a surprising turn of events, Mesa finds himself trying to stay sober. Though he has not yet approached Emil, the need to watch over the young man overwhelms him intensely. Mesa knows he can't do this if his own life is in shambles. A cup of coffee is never far from him and occasionally, it causes sleepless nights, but Mesa is not discouraged. Every morning, as a point of necessity, he examines Paola's case file, hoping to find something new. Mesa walks to the printer and reads the documents that came out.

"Detective Mesa!" A young and chirpy voice greets him. Mesa looks up into bright blue eyes and a grin. It is Taylor, the brightest and youngest officer in the department. For some reason, Taylor always appears happy to Mesa who detests chirpiness. However, he does not find the young chap irritating. Amusement is his primary emotion when it comes to Taylor.

"Taylor. To what do I owe this pleasure?" He asks in his usual sarcastic manner as he casts his gaze back to the report in his hands.

The young officer chuckles, "nothing in particular, I am just happy to see you. I Barely saw you around my first few months here, so seeing you lately in the mornings certainly is nice."

"I'll take that as a compliment."

"Some of the other guys said you and Detective Rivers were planning on retiring soon. So, I thought maybe you were easing yourself into retirement after all these years of hard work," Mesa's head rises slowly as he contemplates Taylor's words. Somehow, the promise he made to Rivers about retirement had totally skipped his mind.

"No, son. Life simply just became tough," Mesa says, his voice hollow

With a nod, Taylor excuses himself, leaving Mesa to his thoughts. The condition he gave, after all for retiring, was resolving Paola's case. Until it is all sorted, he will not bring it up with Rivers, not if he can help it. Someone

suddenly places his hand on his shoulder, startling him,
Speaking of the devil...

"Hey, brother. How are you feeling?" Rivers asks kindly
and Mesa manages a smile as he shrugs his shoulders: "I'm
good, man. How are you? How's the family?"

"All is well, man." Rivers replies as he glances at the report
in Mesa's hands, which prompts him to remember the case
file he just read, and he says to Mesa "Hey, I was just
reading the dead old lady's case file and I just noticed that
two DNA profiles were identified. I'm not sure how that
wasn't mentioned earlier when we were still actively
investigating. One profile came from the old lady's finger
nails and the other was located on the seeds recovered from
her murder scene. The DNA from her nail came back to an
unknown male." Mesa sits up, his attention solely on
Rivers. Rivers continues "the issue is that the second
profile from the seeds belongs to a male with a military
background. It's in CODIS, but because it's in the Navy's
DNA database it can't be accessed by us. The Military does
not provide any information without a court order.

Mesa nods. "I served with a navy Jag attorney I'll reach
out and see what she can do to help. Where was the DNA
found?"

"Next to the old lady, in some seeds or some sort of eating
items. I'll re-check." Rivers says as he starts to leave to
check the case.

"Please go do that now, I'll make a phone call" Mesa says, his heart racing as he reaches for his phone in his pocket. Have they finally found something?

"Hey Stuart, how are things?" Mesa shoots loudly into the phone as the other person picks up.

"Who is this?" A gruff voice responds.

"It's Chief. Mesa. How are you?"

"Mesa! how are you? Have not heard from you in over a decade, man. What can I do for you?" Stuart gets straight to the point as Mesa would.

Mesa excited quickly runs through the details, "We are working a homicide case and we got a DNA hit for a suspect who was probably a sailor, I need to access the Navy's DNA database. I will send a search warrant your way. Keep me posted please."

"Anything for you, Chief," Chief Stuart says promptly.

"Thank you, Chief, and I owe you big time," Mesa ends the call.

When Mesa ends the call, he exhales loudly, feeling excited. Finding DNA is huge and might just be the final key to unlocking whoever perpetrated those crimes. His mind goes to Emil and a smile finds its way to his face. Don't worry, son. We are almost there. Mesa enters his office but pauses at the door. The table is a mess of documents and papers, every time he commits to cleaning it up, something else comes up that distracts him.

"Just might have to do this now," he mutters as he places the report on a chair, ready to clean. A loud knock and a body running into him cause him to jump, startled by the intrusion.

"Dude, what the fuck are you doing? You scared the shit out of me!" Mesa raises his voice at a panting Rivers. His partner shakes his head vigorously in apology.

"Bro, we have another body found in the park. It's a fifteen-year-old girl strangled and sexually assaulted. The lieutenant needs us to handle it. It could be related." Mesa's heart rate picks up at the mention of the word 'related.'

"Related, how?"

"Your business card was found at the scene." Mesa is dumbfounded as he stares at Rivers. His business card? Over the past few months, while investigating the cases, he had given his business card out to so many people. Unless the DNA report comes back with a definite name and person, their job might just have gotten a lot more complicated. The number one problem will be to track all the people, he has handed cards to.

Abandoning the messy table, Mesa says "alright, let's head out." he follows Rivers. Mesa is already wondering how he is going to explain to the family of the assaulted girl what has happened to their daughter. Shaking his head, he decides, I will just leave it to Rivers.

The scene is chaotic. It has been months since the station has had a murder case and everyone is on the ground, doing whatever is necessary. The park is closed, as usual people watch the officers working the crime scene. Mesa's head pounds with excitement and a dull headache. Murder or not, he could feel the familiar stirrings of a case about to be solved. Mesa wonders why the girl was murdered in the park. It's under broad daylight and the murderer stood the risk of exposure. He is getting bolder; Mesa thinks to himself. If the murderer is not caught anytime soon, more gruesome murders will be unearthed.

Beside him, Rivers is talking about the antics of his grandchild, but Mesa is not listening, long gone in thought.

While Rivers continues without noticing Mesa is not listening, "His mother was shocked and then I told her not to panic. I told her she used to do far worse as a kid and it's funny how these kids think they were all well-behaved when they were much younger," Rivers chuckles as they walk into the park. Sometimes, Rivers rambles about happy things when he is nervous. Mesa cannot tell if this is one of such times.

A burly man with a baldhead walks towards them; He introduces himself "Gentlemen, hope all is well. I'm

Detective Marshall." extending his hand out for handshakes.

"Hey, brother. Thanks for the call. I'm Rivers and this is my partner, Mesa." Mesa nods at him as he grips his hand firmly.

"Nice to meet you, gents. Glad you could make it here in time. Follow me over here." The man gestures forward and the detectives move quickly behind him, eager to see what lies ahead.

"Detectives, the deceased is Hayti Jones. Fifteen years old and she was strangled on her way to school. She was found by a jogger earlier today." Marshall explains, pointing to a body that is being put into a bag. The girl's hair is platinum blonde and Mesa stares at it, wondering what a young girl could have done to deserve such a violent death.

"My partner received information that your reporting officers found my business card next to the body," Mesa blurts out, turning to face Marshall who nods vigorously.

"That's correct. The card was found within arm's reach. It's been raining the past few days and both the card, and the body are dry and clean: that makes it more likely that may be connected. A witness believes she saw a homeless guy in the park near the area before the body was discovered. She was able to see his face."

"Any CCTV or tag reader in the area? We have to recanvas the area for additional witnesses," Mesa says softly as he pauses to stare at the body being put into the bag. There are no visible scratches around her neck. Mesa glances at her fingertips, hopefully, something will come up in the forensic analysis. As he examines the body, something moves sharply at the outskirts of scene and he catches it from the corner of his eye. When he looks up, he sees a homeless man peeking behind a tree at them. Careful not to let him suspect a thing, Mesa rises.

"We have a spectator, that possibly matches the witness statement" he announces calmly, causing Marshall to raise an eyebrow in question. Rivers turns inconspicuously.

"Ten-four," He replies calmly. Mesa keeps his face on the body.

"You flank the right and I'll go straight to him," Rivers says to Mesa who nods. Marshall watches as the partners make their move.

"We move as normally as possible, so we don't startle him into a run," Mesa says from the corner of his mouth.

Mesa risks a quick glance at the possible suspect, but is still unable to get a clear view of his face. As Mesa and Rivers make their way toward him, the homeless person realizes he has been spotted. Without missing a beat, he turns around and flees. Rivers and Mesa double up, chasing after him with Marshall barking orders to the officers on the scene. Mesa runs as fast as he can, tailing their suspect but he moves faster than Mesa and he loses sight of him.

Rivers barks into his radio "we are in a foot pursuit! A white male wearing a purple shirt and light-colored shorts. Medium length brown hair and about 5'9" in height. I need some uniforms to roll our way, be advised we are in plain clothes". In less than a minute, cruisers zoom past, and they set up a cordon around the area. It seems the homeless man has disappeared into thin air.

"Where is he?" Marshall asks as he steps out of a cruiser to a panting Mesa.

"Haven't spotted him yet," Mesa pants, holding his chest. Running is soon becoming an old pastime. It takes Mesa a minute to catch his breath before joining the other officers in searching the area.

"He couldn't have gone far. Perhaps we should retrace our steps," Rivers is saying to another officer.

"He's probably hiding but where?" Mesa mutters to himself. That's when he sees it. Quietly, he whistles a familiar tune, and Rivers turns, inching towards him at once. Mesa nods towards a car, causing Rivers to smile.

"Gentlemen, I guess that's it. He's gone and there's nothing we can do," Rivers yells in a loud voice as he and Mesa approach the parked car.

"Let's all just relax and head back," Mesa yells, nodding towards the car. The officers hold their guns close as Mesa and Rivers inch closer. In one quick move, the two men double over and pull out the man from underneath the car.

"Freeze!" Mesa yells but he's the one who is suddenly frozen in place.

"Oh… no." Rivers chuckles nervously.

"I'm sorry for running. I'm sorry. I saw the lights, cars, and body and thought it was my baby."

Mesa sighs as he stares at the young man, unbelieving. He looks less scruffy than Mesa remembered with his face looking cleaner and even his hair is shorter. He must have gotten a shower, Mesa thinks to himself as he stands to his feet, taking a few steps backward so Emil can stand.

"It's okay, guys. It's someone we know," Mesa yells at the officers, trying to get them to leave especially Marshall who is scrutinizing them heavily. "There's nothing to worry about, guys. Please go back to the scene," Mesa says with a smile, trying to be convincing and it works. When they're finally alone, Mesa turns to glare at Emil.

"I know I'm getting close to finding her or whoever took her," Emil murmurs, causing Mesa to rub his eyes wearily.

"Emil, you have to stop. Let's us do the work and just go home." Emil's face suddenly contorts in anger, glaring at Mesa.

"Do the work, you say. Do you? Are you really doing the work?" He barks with emotion. "Look at me, Detective. Look how much suffering I have endured, and you tell me that it works. The fucking system does not care if the citizens are being killed, raped kidnapped. All they care about is a moment of glory, a chance to be a judge and you stand here and tell me not to worry!" He yells. He rises slowly and with all the strength he can muster, he pushes Mesa.

"Get the fuck away from me!" He screams. Detective Rivers is alarmed.

"That's how you repay us for working tireless hours trying to find your daughter?" Rivers says to Emil then glances at Mesa, pissed. "Fuck us, that's basically what the fuck he is saying!"

Mesa remains quiet as he stares at the two of them. When he does not respond, Rivers gets infuriated and he moves closer to Emil, grabbing his arm.

"Motherfucker, place your hands behind your back for assaulting an officer"

Mesa quickly grabs Rivers, "Partner, he is right, Let him go." The two officers stare at each other, Emil glances between the two of them. Reluctantly, Rivers releases Emil's arm but he gives him the stink eye. Emil huffs at Rivers as he shakes his arm.

"Ask your partner what happened the last time I trusted the system," He mutters quietly before stalking off. Mesa watches him, his chest heavy but he decides against calling him back. Emil has every right to be upset with them. The system. Everyone.

"We should go, Mesa. We should leave." Rivers sounds pissed.

The two detectives walk quietly back towards their cruiser, each man deep in thought. Mesa wonders if Emil had seen the perpetrator of the murder. An odd thought equally occurs to him. What if Emil was the perpetrator? Worried about his line of thinking, Mesa exhales, shaking the thought out of his mind. Rivers glances at Mesa but does not say a thing, several thoughts running through his mind. When they arrive at the cruiser, without saying goodbye to the officers, the two men simply leave with Rivers driving. Two minutes into the drive Rivers unable to contain it anymore blurts out, "What was that about?"

"What was what about?" Mesa asks, confused.

"The whole conversation with Emil. I just thought you took a liking to him, and that the case was just a coincidental one that really moved you. What did he mean by all that?" Mesa sighs as he sinks lower into the seat, unwilling to tell the story. However, he decides to tell it.

"I knew him as a boy. He was young and an adorable little thing. His case was one of the first cases I worked. His stepfather sexually abused him as a child." Rivers interrupt mesa quick inhale and soft swearing, "The hell, what kind of father does that?"

"A bastard stepfather. Anyways, we arrested him but the first time: the mom was in denial, the prosecutor that bitch Ricks was on a seeking supervisor mission and the kid was

138

on his own and cornered that right on the stand he became so terrified that he recounted his story and said he lied, although evidence was clear that he had told the truth, but nobody gave a fuck. Shit bag stepfather goes free and mom of course still in denial lets him back home with the kids and the shitbag does it again. This time mom can't pretend and the shitbag get arrested I've never felt more terrible in my life," Mesa mutters miserably.

"And the mother?"

"A fucking waste of space. I do not know why she acted the way she did. She never verbally expressed any thought about it, but it was obvious that she was on the man's side. A couple of times, I wished she was a man, so I could put one or two blows through her skull," Mesa replies bitterly as Rivers shakes his head.

"The poor kid must have been traumatized. Damn. Imagine not being supported by your mother," Rivers says in a distant voice, voicing out thoughts Mesa has had for years.

"I tried to reach out to the kid after the case, but the Chief wouldn't let me.

"Wow. That's messed up. That's beyond messed up." Rivers says.

"So, the poor kid had a hard time believing anyone. I even promised him a safe happy home but before I could open my eyes, Child Services took him away, and locating him became extremely difficult."

"But what in the hell happened to the stepfather? Is he still in prison?" Rivers asked

Rumor has it that a guard name Ogando, put the word out that he was a child molester, and the other inmates took care of the problem, justice served. Ultimately, the mother committed suicide leaving the children to the state.

"And then his daughter gets taken away," Rivers muses as Mesa repeats and "then his daughter gets taken away."

"Now, it makes more sense why you've been so focused on this case."

"Exactly. That is why I want us to solve this case, Rivers. I need the peace and closure it will bring me but more importantly, Emil needs it."

River stays quiet as they drive to the station. Mesa adjusts the car seat and lowers himself backward, placing his hands on his stomach to stare at the ceiling. Sometimes, he wonders if life would be a lot simpler if he had chosen an easy path; if he was married with kids and he had decided to be a stay-at-home Dad for his kids.

However, nothing ever really is easy. Everything comes at a price.

CHAPTER 12

Ever since Mesa told him Emil's story, Rivers finds himself being more introspective, ruminating on his own childhood. His mother was quick to always blame him and hit him. Thankfully, she was checked into a mental institution early enough before she could cause some severe damage to him. At odd moments, a picture of Emil pops into his head, and he pauses to reflect on the young man's case. Rivers is thankful he at least has his wife to discuss things with, Mesa has no one to share his own thoughts with. At some point Rivers thought his partner was spiraling out of control because he was sad to leave the force and the reason why he refused to talk about retirement. The loud ring of the phone startles Rivers out of his thoughts and he quickly reaches for the phone.

"Rivers."

"Hey," The familiar voice of Detective Marshall fills his ears. "The narcotics unit just arrested a mailman who was delivering Khat to an Ethiopian restaurant and claims that he has information that could help with Paola's case and Rivers... hurry the fuck up before the Feds come get this dude." Rising to his feet, Rivers starts to make his way towards Mesa's office next door.

"Thanks, man. We are on our way," he says loudly, drawing Mesa's attention.

"What's up?" Mesa asks, as Rivers ends the call.

"Narcotics arrested a mailman who has information about Paola's case." Mesa jumps to his feet, his eyes wide and excited. Rivers smiles, happy to see his partner excited. He makes a mental note to take him to dinner when it's all over. Mesa probably has not had a decent meal in days.

"Let's go." Mesa says, already walking towards the door.

"Certainly," Rivers chuckles as Mesa moves fast out of his office and Rivers tails him. When they were much younger, Mesa used to walk extremely fast and he found it difficult to keep up with the tall man but now, his partner moves slower. They certainly aren't getting any younger.

On the walk to the Narcotics unit Rivers makes small talk, "Had lunch yet, Mesa?" His partner shakes his head no.

"How about we stop at Nialles Diner for burgers, after this? We haven't had lunch together in a while," he says jovially and Mesa's face softens considerably.

"That's true. I suppose it's all been the work stress of recent."

"True, plus my health. If my wife ever finds out I'm eating burgers, she will have my head. I've been put on a strictly vegan diet," he sighs dramatically.

"That doesn't sound fun, is that even possible for you?" Mesa chuckles.

"Well, I'm a man under feminine authority. I have no choice but to obey her." Rivers says in a mockingly defeated voice.

The Narcotics Unit is on the other side of the station and is a two-minute walk from their offices. The unit buzzes with activity as Mesa and Rivers step in. A couple of kids are seated against the wall and from their buzzed faces; Rivers knows they have been brought in for handling drugs.

"Sergeant Mike," Mesa calls loudly ahead and a big Mexican guy turns around with a huge smile on his face.

"Oh, look! It's two of my favorite detectives!" He laughs as he pulls Mesa into a big bear hug. Reluctantly, Mesa allows himself to be hugged. When Mike pulls away from Mesa, he pulls Rivers in too. Rivers is rewarded with several back pats before Mike lets him go.

"We heard you have a mailman in custody who can help with our case," Mesa says urgently, impatience clouding his eyes. Mike laughs, hitting his arm gently.

"You're still as impatient as ever. Aren't you going to ask about me? How I'm doing?" Mike teases, hitting his arm again. Rivers can see the impatience unfurling across Mesa's face and he chuckles.

"You know Mesa, Mike. He is always ready to get down to business. Let him be." Rivers mocks.

Sgt. Mike laughs and gets to business, "yes, yes, I do have a mailman in custody. He was delivering Khat to

143

Ethiopians in DC and he was stopped with several pounds of Khat. He refused to speak about the Khat but stated that he could help us with a murder that occurred a while ago. We searched the database and discovered that you are the lead on the case, detective," He nods at Mesa.

"Okay. Where is he now?" says Mesa anxiously, needing to get some answers.

"In the interrogation room. Right, this way." Mike leads the way, and the detectives follow. The two detectives enter the viewing room to observe the suspect. Upon entering the room, Mesa inspects the mailman keenly. He is wearing a mailman uniform, leaning forward with both elbows resting on his knees. From the unbothered look on his face, Mesa can tell that he's noticeably confident.

"I guess I'll leave you guys to it then," Mike says rubbing their shoulders simultaneously before excusing himself. The two detectives watch in silence, sizing the mailman up.

"What do you think? Think he's involved in the crimes himself?", Rivers asks.

Mesa stays pensive looking at the man and then says "let's find out." He takes a deep breath and asks, "So how are we doing this?"

"Let's go in, you interview and I read body language," responds Rivers.

"Sounds good, let's go" Mesa says leading the way.

River's hands turn sweaty for the first time in years, and he feels nervous: if they close this case, they can certainly talk about retirement. Please go well, Rivers prays within himself. When Mesa opens the door, Rivers puts on a serious face, game time.

The mailman looks up as the two detectives walk in, looking serious. The investigation room is sparse with just a table, a couple of chairs and a few dimly lit bulbs. The mailman's appearance is very ordinary, freckles litter his face, his arms are thin and long, and his ears are huge for the size of his face.

"Good afternoon, sir, I'm Detective Mesa and this is Detective Rivers," Mesa says pointing at Rivers. "It is my understanding that you have some information that could assist us in the disappearance of Paola, yes?"

"Yeahhh!"

"Okay, let's hear it." The mailman places hands together and rubs them together, smirking proudly.

"What I need to hear is MONEY AND DEAL!" He chuckles as he winks at them. "I wanna click my heels three times and go home, you feel me?" He licks his lips before leaning backwards, a smirk on his face. Mesa and Rivers glance at each other, a knowing look in their eyes.

"Money and Deal? Three times, huh?" Mesa asks slyly, folding his arms on the table.

There is a moment of silence, and the mailman glances between the two men. His face suddenly hardens. "Man, don't play stupid, I want the reward and these charges to go away, BROTHER!"

Mesa nods his head calmly, "Sir, unfortunately, we can't promise you anything. We can only give you money as a form of payment if you are an informant or if your information leads to an arrest and sentencing..."

"Oh okay. So, I guess you're not getting shit from me, and that little bitch will stay gone..." The mailman intones, glaring at them. Mesa begins to chuckle as he glances at Rivers. Detective Mesa slams both hands on the table, startling them all.

"Don't you fucking dare call her a bitch, you mother fucker!" Mesa yells in his face but Rivers grabs his arm, pulling him back into his chair. The vein on mesa's forehead is visibly prominent as the mailman stares at him, shocked at his sudden transformation.

Mesa continues, "you are going to be sucking dicks and rubbing dudes' backs by the time I finish with my report, detailing your full cooperation with the police, better yet, child abductor. You go in as Nestor and come out as Dorothy, can you hear the three heels click, BROTHER?!" His dark threat hangs in the air as he tries to regain composure. Rivers steps in, worried that things might escalate.

"Partner, I got it," he mutters to Mesa, placing his hand briefly on his shoulder. Nestor looks slightly shaken but his face is scrunched up as if he is mustering all the courage he has left.

Rivers says in a sarcastic monotone, "Sir, you are absolutely right, the charges need to go away, and you deserve money. I understand that the AUSA would probably make a deal with you, as they always do, but we are not going to ask for one. Let me tell you what we will do, as a favor to you."

In anticipation, Nestor leans in, his eyes widening with greed, "I'm listening."

Rivers continues, "you are obstructing justice by refusing to provide vital information on a child abduction. You could possibly be charged as an accessory after the fact. I am going to help you out. I'm going to notify the US Postal Service Police to charge you with a felony for utilizing a government vehicle while transporting narcotics. Then, I'm going to notify the DEA and ask them to run your vehicle GPS and locate all your Ethiopian friends to whom you delivered Khat. To top it off, I'm calling the fucking FBI and let them charge you with the child exportation act BROTHER! Now, ask yourself, are you a witness or are you a fucking defendant!" Rivers ends with a dramatic flourish.

Mesa watches the shadow flit across Nestor's face. Rivers words may have been delivered quietly but they had a tremendous effect, and Nestor's lower lip begins to quiver.

Aware of Nestor's gaze on him, Mesa ecstatic rises and heads towards the door. He opens the interview room door and shouts at an officer busy peering into a file, "Lawrence, take this piece of shit to central booking and make sure that his file says "child abductor." Quickly, Lawrence makes his way into the Investigation room with a menacing look on his face, but Nestor is already on his feet, panic in his eyes as he chuckles nervously.

"Hold on, man, I was just playing with you. Hear me out, okay?" Lawrence glances at Mesa, his eyebrow in question, and Mesa nods, a sign that he can leave. When the door closes behind Lawrence, Nestor starts to talk.

"I was making a delivery in front of the house where the girl went missing and before I got out of the van, I saw the little girl looking for a dog or a cat or some shit like that. She went to the rear of her home and the white boy next door followed her.. I recorded the whole thing because I knew he was up to no good, you know what I'm saying," Mesa watches as Nestor reaches for his phone in his pocket. In less than a minute, he taps play on the phone and hands it to the Detectives. The two men watch as the camera zooms in on a small Paola, calling for her cat. A few seconds later, a man tiptoes carefully behind her. That is when it hits Mesa, the man he gave his business card to.

How did he not see this? When he glances at Rivers, he can tell that his partner is thinking the same thing.

Anger floods Mesa's veins and he pictures strangling the life out of Nestor. After all this fucking time!" And why didn't you come forward with this months ago? Why wait so long?" Mesa says with a choked voice, his fingers balled into fists. Nestor steps back, worried about the murderous look in Mesa's eyes.

"Come on man, I-I-I"

"Shut the fuck up!" Mesa says and signals to Rivers, the two men hurry out of the room with the cell phone towards Mesa's office.

"Don't leave me here! What's going to happen to me?" Nestor shouts anxiously.

Nestor's video leaves the two detectives feeling motivated, especially Mesa. Though he mentioned Ben, nothing in the video explicitly says that Ben kidnapped Paola especially since there is no further footage. All the photographs from the scene are scattered across Mesa's desk with Rivers going over each of them one after the other and Mesa staring at his board. They need a concrete piece of evidence, something, anything. They both spent the night in the station trying to find the one piece of evidence they need to make the case.

Nestor is still in custody, Mesa racks his mind thoroughly, wondering if there's any question, he didn't ask the man, but nothing comes to mind. Rivers drags himself to his side, resisting a yawn while he stares at Mesa's board.

"So, what now?" Rivers yawns.

"The video just shows him walking to the yard and nothing else. We have one chance to get this motherfucker," Mesa exhales, craving something he has wanted in a long time as he moves towards his table and lightly drops a file on the table.

"I can't even remember the last time we stayed up this long," Rivers, yawns again.

Years ago. The Radcliffe case, I suppose," Mesa replies, rubbing his neck. He had dozed off at the wrong angle and now his neck won't stop creaking. "Either way, it's been a while. I cannot wait to go home after this. My back hurts like hell. Man, I feel like I need a fucking cigarette. I don't even smoke anymore," he murmurs as he rubs his tired eyes, settling into his chair. Rivers remains standing staring at the board. Mesa leans back into his chair so he can prop his feet on the table, his mind wonders where he can get a cigarette. Although he no longer smokes, he keeps a box of cigarettes in his car glove compartment next to an old pack of sunflower seeds that he never remembered to throw out. Sunflower seeds... cigarette, that's it. "Fucking cigarette!" Mesa yells as his legs come crashing to the ground and he rushes towards the board while Rivers stares at him, confused. Mesa grabs a marker and begins to scribble furiously across the board.

"What's going on, Mesa? Run me through your thought process," Rivers says impatiently and Mesa turns to him with the familiar excitement of a case that is about to be solved.

"So, all four murders and the disappearing happened within eleven months, correct?"

"Correct!" Rivers responds.

"Sunflower seeds were located in the murder of the old lady after Paola, right? All the murders have the same M.O! Young, white females going to school!" Mesa says urgently but between his fatigue and hunger, Rivers is confused and does not get it

"Bro, where are you going with this?"

"Don't you see? It's him! He did it! That son of a bitch was in front of us all this time!"

Rivers blinks. "Who did it?" Detective Mesa grabs a piece of paper underneath the stack of pictures on his table and hands it to Rivers, his eyes glistening with excitement.

"Don't you see, the day Paola disappeared, when we interviewed him, he said he never saw the child that morning, but we clearly just saw video that shows he lied. In his written statement he described her as a girl and later, he asked us if we had found the woman: when he first observed her, she was a child after he kidnapped her she was a girls because he had a sexual desire for her and then after he sexually assaulted her she became a woman to him. Unconsciously he told us the truth, but we didn't notice it. The fucking K9 was right, that's where the dog alerted." Before Rivers could processes and respond, Mesa grabs his cellphone and starts to dial a number immediately.

"This is absolutely crazy," Rivers murmurs.

Mesa nods, "it certainly is, I do not know how we did not see it before, Rivers. It was literally right there, staring us in the face."

"We've been doing our best, Mesa."

"Chief Stuart, I need you to run that DNA sample against my DNA stored in the military database," Mesa says quickly. Immediately, he puts the phone on the loudspeaker.

"What?" asks Chief Stuart confused.

"Chief, trust me, I need you to trust me on this one.

"Okay, hold on." There is a moment of silence, and the two detectives share a look.

Rivers is still confused; he doesn't understand why Mesa is making the request but through the years he has learned to trust his partner.

"What do you think it's going to be?" Rivers mouths to Mesa who shrugs, not ready to say his thoughts aloud.

"It's a match, it's your DNA." Chief Stuarts's voice pierces the quiet room and Mesa closes his eyes briefly as relief washes over him and he thinks, I got him.

"Please email me the results. I will explain later. And Chief? Thank you!" Mesa says genuinely.

"No problem."

When Mesa ends the call, Rivers in shock to hear that the DNA from a crime scene comes back to his partner demands to know what is going on. Mesa explains: The canine took us to the Ben's shed, the same shed I spit sunflower seeds in, and then sunflower seeds with my DNA were recovered in the old lady scene, not far from Ben's house. Have we been able to identify the old lady? We need to know how she is connected to Ben.

Rivers states, "I'm on it, I think I had just gotten a return right before Narcotics called to tell me about Nestor." Let me go to my office and check.

A few minutes later Rivers walks back into Mesa's office, quiet and astonished and says, "partner the vehicle found running, and the deceased old lady are one of the same: Yolanda Smith, Ben Smith's sister."

Mesa puts his hand out and Rivers meets him for a high-five.

"We got him. We finally got him," Rivers says soberly and his partner nods, It has finally come to an end.

"I'll get the search warrant and you notify SWAT," Mesa says quietly.

"Immediately," Rivers says, before bolting out of the room in excitement. Mesa stares at the board, feeling terrible. After all this time, the murderer has been staring him in the face without blinking. Mesa leans against his table and sighs. Why did he do such a thing? Did Emil hurt him or his family?

****

Today is going to be a good day, Ben woke up with that thought in his head and a spring in his step. Whatever good it is, he cannot wait to know what it is. The sky is clear and blue, adding to the good feeling that Ben has. The weather is cool, and Ben decides to take advantage of it. He grabs his lawn mower and pulls it out, whistling quietly. Ever since his last escapade, he has been feeling a lot more energetic, an adrenaline high. As he tries to switch on the lawn mower, he glances over at his neighbor's house. It has been several months and there has been no sign of either Emil or Caitlin. The lawn is busy and tall plants surround the house. Ben shakes his head sadly. He was hoping they would stick around longer.

Somewhere nearby, there is the distant sound of Nina singing and Ben nods along. The thought of his next victim keeps him mentally occupied as he mows the lawn with a smile. Her neck was looking especially luscious and attractive. The feeling of bones crushing underneath his fingers makes his eyes roll back into his head.

The sound of a car driving past causes Ben to come out of his thoughts and to look up, bringing a sinical smile to his lips, he knew this was going to happen. Leading a procession of police cars is Detective Rivers and Detective Mesa. Neither of the men look pleased, sporting grim looks on their faces. Ben continues mowing, nodding his head along with the music playing. The sound of car doors slamming is like a metallic symphony and the sound of their feet against the pavement is the horrific percussion.

"Welcome, welcome. I've been expecting you for a while now," Ben says as he bends to turn off the lawn mower.

"Get on your knees! Show me your hands!" A man yells in his face, pointing a gun at him as the other officer's advance behind him, holding their guns. Ben raises his hands slowly.

"About time, Detectives, many bumps in the road, my poor sister noticed before the police. What was it, what gave me away, my smile?" No one responds to him, instead, the officers gather around him and handcuff his hands. The sinister smile never leaves his face.

"Where you are going, a smile and lips will take you far," Mesa sneers and Ben snorts, a snide comment threatens to leave his lips but he holds it in. There is a dark look in the detective's eyes and Ben wonders what he is thinking.

"Clear," SWAT members yell as they are strategically entering Ben's house. Ben watches as the detectives converse among themselves, moving around the house.

"There's nothing for you to see, Detectives," Ben yells but he is ignored as they pull him violently towards a cruiser. In the house opposite his, his intended next victim stands on her porch, her mouth open in shock. Ben's smile widens as he winks at her. Another time, love.

Behind Ben, Mesa is pacing back and forth, trying to remember something. When a bulb goes on in his head, he rushes into Ben's backyard, the other officers on his tail; with force, he pulls open the shed doors and is greeted with a cement ground. This is it, when Rivers steps into the shed, he sighs.

"Damn. There was no way anyone would have picked this up if we didn't have all of those clues."

"Call the fire department, what we need is under the cement," Mesa says to the officer behind Rivers.

Mesa and Rivers share a look, "this man is a bastard," Rivers mutters as Mesa kneels, touching the concrete ground lightly.

"He totally is. Only God knows how he managed all this while Emil and his family were next doors," Mesa exhales as his chest beats wildly, eager to unearth the mystery underneath.

Hearing the fire truck sirens approaching, Rivers suggests, "let's go back to search the house, the fire department will have this done in minutes" and Mesa agrees, following behind him with another two officers. Ben's house is barely spectacular. The house is sparse with just two couches and a small table in the kitchen. It's the classic living condition for a psychopathic serial killer. There is nothing in the house to arouse suspicion.

"Search everywhere," Mesa informs the others.

The officers move quickly, checking the rooms for any sign of life. Minutes into their search, Mesa gets a phone call.

"Detectives, we found a body."

Pulling Rivers with him, the men hurry out of the house and back into the backyard. Mesa stops in his tracks upon entering the shed, staring at what was unearthed. Tucked into the earth is a body bags. With a careful hand, Mesa reaches down and unzips the bag. It reveals the decomposed body of Paola still wearing the school uniform in which she was last seen. Mesa sighs, tears springing surprisingly to his eyes.

"Time to bring you home," He murmurs.

Rising slowly, Mesa walks out of the shed, leaving the other men there. Mesa's gaze lands on Emil's abandoned house. The house is always going to be haunted by memories of his daughter.

"What are you thinking?" Rivers asks as he appears beside Mesa. The detective shrugs.

"How living in that house will be rather difficult for the family. The best thing they can do is to sell the house and start fresh somewhere else." River nods in agreement, "it's the only way."

"Let's go, Rivers. Our work here is done," Mesa's voice is forlorn and withdrawn. Mesa walks slowly with his shoulders slumped even though the heavy load of the case has finally been removed from his shoulders.

When Mesa walks out of the backyard unto the lawn, Emil is standing across the street with questions in his eyes.

The scent of chicken wafts in the air and Emil is reminded of the nights they all spent in the house together with Caitlin grilling chicken in the kitchen. Those were happy times. Those were fun times. Paola particularly asked several times for chicken nights to be made an everyday tradition.

"Eating chicken every day is probably not healthy," Emil had told her one night. His wife scoffed.

"Probably? You need more vegetables than chicken, young lady, and I'd advise you to eat those greens immediately," Caitlin warned. A smile graces Emil's lips as the memory fizzles out. They had a good run as a family.

The streets are empty. Earlier, it was littered with police cars. Emil watched as the detectives searched Ben's house.

He stood across the street, wondering what the problem could be. When Ben was put in handcuffs, Emil began to panic. The moment Mesa came into view, Emil's feet began to find their way across, seeking an explanation.

"Sir, get back!" An officer yelled when he approached, but Mesa told the officer to let him through.

"What's happening? Is Ben safe?" Emil asked anxious.

"Emil, we found your daughter's body, I'm sorry." The words hit Emil like a heavy weight, and he loses all feeling in his legs, hitting the ground. Ben? Ben, who helped him and comforted him during his worst moments? Ben brought him food and gave him counsel on the difficult days when Caitlin was beyond miserable. His body curled in shock as he stared at the grass, hugging himself.

"I'm sorry, baby. I am sorry for not protecting you. I'm sorry, baby," Emil muttered to himself. Tears did not come, instead his body was left in a state of shock. Mesa leaned down and wrapped his arms around him. Emil has no idea how long he sat on the grass but when he got up, with the Mesa's help, most of the officers were gone.

Emil asks how? Why? He has so many questions, he doesn't even know where to start doesn't know what to ask. Mesa says, "I know there is a lot you need and want to know but right now we are still putting the pieces together. I promise, I will have better answers for you tomorrow. Please you and Caitlin come to my office tomorrow any time. I'll be there and we can sit down, and I'll tell you everything I can. Call me if you need anything at all, okay?"

Emil buries his head in his hands, sighing. There was only one person he wanted to call when Mesa gave him the news. He doesn't remember walking; he didn't even know that he was going there until he heard the voice.

"Emil?"

Emil looks up into his wife's eyes. Concern clouds her face as she assesses his face and dirt-stricken body. She's as beautiful as always, dressed in a lilac dress and shoes to match.

"Is everything okay?"

He hears himself respond, he sounds far away; "Oh, yeah. Everything is...fine...Actually, it is not. She is dead, she has been dead for months," Emil announces with that hollow voice he doesn't recognize. He stares at Caitlin's feet, unable to look in her eyes and see the pain in them, he continues without pausing, knowing that if he does, he will lose his courage. "The police discovered her body today."

Caitlin makes no move but when he finally looks into her face, her hand is covering her mouth, and tears stream down her face.

"It gets worse. She was taken by Ben, Ben our neighbor." A gasp escapes Caitlin as she starts to sway on her feet in shock, the blood from her face draining in horror and disbelief.

"Ben our neighbor?" She whispers, Emil nods, suddenly unable to stand still, he shakes his legs gently to keep them from buckling from the pain he feels. Caitlin lets out a deep moan as she clutches her stomach. Unable to help himself, Emil reaches for her, and the two hug tightly, weeping against one another.

"I wanted to be wrong, I prayed, I hoped " Caitlin wails unable to finish her words, clutching to Emil for dear life. The two weep for themselves, for their daughter and the realization that all hope of her being alive is gone. They weep for the years she lived and those she didn't get a chance to. They weep for the time they spent together and the time they wasted because of their differences in opinions, that seem so mundane now.

"I'm so sorry for not going with you, Caitlin. I just couldn't---" Caitlin's finger cuts him off as she refuses to let him finish.

"There's nothing to apologize for, Emil. I am the one who should be apologizing. I gave up to early and I blamed you. Imagine that! The man who loved our daughter the most is the person I blamed. I'm so sorry," Caitlin sniffs as she wipes the tears off Emil's face with her bare hands.

"There's nothing to be sorry about, Caitlin. Nothing."

The two hug each other tightly again, grieving deeply in each other's arms.

"It's all over now, darling. It's all over," He soothes as he rubs her back.

CHAPTER 13

"In the book of Romans reads - Therefore, those in union with Christ Jesus have no condemnation. For the law of the spirit that gives life in union with Christ Jesus has set you free from the law of sin and of death. What the Law was incapable of doing because it was weak through the flesh, God did by sending his own Son in the likeness of sinful flesh and concerning sin, condemning sin in the flesh, so that the righteous requirement of the Law might be fulfilled in us who walk, not according to the flesh, but according to the spirit."

Father Vernon drones on, speaking about life, death, and resurrection, Emil hears the words but he is not listening, Paola's grave is all he can focus on. Occasionally, his attention drifts to Caitlin's hand which is wrapped in his right hand. It's been far too long, and they shouldn't have been apart for even a day. Though his wife's eyes are dry, Emil can feel the pain coursing through her, and he wishes he hadn't misunderstood her. She's a mother, her maternal instinct was right. She probably knew the day Ben murdered Paola. She said it to him, the day she felt the connection between her and Paola was severed but she had no way of explaining it to him. As he stares at his daughter's tombstone, Emil knows he will never forget her, but he will heal, he will do it for Caitlin and Jr.

Caitlin squeezes his hand suddenly, drawing his attention. Father Vernon is staring at him in question.

"Do you have anything to say, Emil?" Emil shakes his head. There's nothing left to be said.

"Caitlin?" Caitlin gives the same response as her husband and Father Vernon bows his head to pray. Emil zones out again, Father Vernon's words are a distant sound. When Caitlin squeezes his hand again, Father Vernon is making his way out of the cemetery and her eyes are shining with tears.

"It's finally over, Emil. It's all over," she whispers. He wants to say It is not over, Caitlin, instead he pulls her in for a hug; she has a new scent on, it's a mist of Jasmine and rosemary. When she pulls back, he holds her face in his hands, and whispers passionately to her "Caitlin, I just want you to know that I love you and our kids beyond life itself and if anyone or anything threatens the life we have together: I won't stop till they're gone from our lives," he leans in to place a kiss on her head and pulls Jr. into their embrace.

Caitlin blinks rapidly, looking at something behind Emil. "That kind policeman is here again," she nods towards him. Mesa is loitering near the cemetery's gate, staring at the couple.

"I'm not sure why he's here," Emil says hesitantly but Caitlin squeezes his hand.

"Let's go. It's probably an update about the case or something similar." She pulls him and Jr. along gently.

Mesa shoves his hands into his pockets as they approach, and Emil can see that he is slightly nervous.

"Detective, thank you for all your help, dedication, and commitment to my family and our baby." Emil puts his hand out and Mess takes it quickly, looking serious.

"It was my pleasure, sir, and once again, sorry for your loss." There is a strange look in his eyes similar to pity but not quite. Emil squeezes Caitlin's hands.

"Baby, can you give us a minute?" Caitlin kisses Emil on the cheek gently.

"Okay, and thank you, detective," Caitlin says softly before leaving the two men to talk. There's a brief moment of silence. Mesa looks like he has something to say but decides against it.

"So, how's the case coming along?" asks Emil.

Mesa responds quickly, "well, the mail man, Nestor, was offered a plea deal and is currently in high supervision, GPS release. We are monitoring him and if he messes up again, he will do hard time."

"Wow, and is he allowed to work in the postal services?" asks Emil discontent.

"No, he is working midnights in the trash company, on the northeast side."

Emil nods, glancing at a tombstone nearby, trying to reign in his emotions. The question he aches to ask is arousing certain levels of anger he finds dangerous.

"Ben?" He manages to ask, his voice shaky. If Mesa noticed, he does not say a thing. Instead, his face becomes a blank canvas.

"He is awaiting trial in DC jail, and…, it's confirmed, he strangled his sister because one way or another she figured it out. We matched the sunflower seeds to the ones I left on his shed. He also dropped a business card, that I gave him at another scene with his DNA on it. Can't figure out if he left all that evidence deliberately or carelessly.

"Okay. Well, detective, thank you," Emil puts his hand out again for another handshake and Mesa takes it, gripping it firmly.

"How are you holding up? Your wife ?" Emil shrugs, avoiding his scrutinizing gaze.

"We're managing. It has not been easy. Finding her body was just like opening an old wound but that is the thing with old wounds, the scar is always there.

"And your son?"

"He's coping, healing alongside his parents. We're all in the new house my wife got. We'll sell the old house soon."

"It's a brilliant plan. I hope it all goes well."

"It most certainly will. Thank you for everything, Detective." Emil puts his hand out and the Mesa grabs it, shaking it firmly, and this time, Mesa hugs Emil as tears run down his face.

"And don't forget, if you ever need---"

"Anything, I should call you. I did not forget. I remembered your words very clearly. Can I call you if I get a ticket though?" Emil teases, causing Mesa to chuckle.

"Don't get a ticket. If you do, the best I can do is to follow you to court and yell 'forgive him' to the judge. That wouldn't be helpful now, would it?" Mesa smiles ruefully as Emil pretends to pout.

"I suppose I'm all alone then. Have a nice day, detective." Emil responds sarcastically and Mesa catches on quickly, amused especially by Emil's antics.

"Have a nice day, Emil. My regards to your wife, okay?" The two men walk to their individual cars, both seemingly at peace and calm. Emil allows Caitlin to hug him one more time.

****

"Drinks on me!" Mesa chuckles as River lugs in a pack of beer, excitement in his eyes. Since they left Ben's house, Rivers wouldn't shut up about the case.

"How did we not see it, Mesa? He was literally under our nose! He must have been plotting those deaths for so long!"

For Mesa, arresting Ben was very therapeutic, it lifted the invisible weight, which had kept his shoulders tight with tension and his chest as heavy as a rock. Mesa could finally breathe again. Finally, he paid his debt and cleared his tab with Emil. The pain in the young man's eyes earlier was gut-wrenching. He was betrayed by someone he couldn't have seen coming.

"Are we celebrating or not?" Rivers yells at Mesa who shakes his head with a small smile.

"Yes, we are celebrating but hold on. First, we must go back to where it all began." Mesa walks towards the murder board. The board is an eclectic mix of photographs, names, and article pieces among many others with several lines joining different pieces together. With a marker, he writes CLOSED on the victims' names and photos. Across Ben's picture, he writes ARRESTED. Mesa stares at the board with satisfaction.

"Looks good, doesn't it?" Rivers says behind him and Mesa nods in agreement. It's a messy yet beautiful board of victory.

"Thankfully. Ben will feel the full wrath of the law," Rivers adds again.

"Now, I can rest," says mesa.

"Now, WE can rest, Mesa. It's not just you who has been in this long haul" says Rivers.

Mesa smiles ruefully. "ok, ok, partner, sorry about that, WE can rest." There is a knock on the door and the two men turn to stare at the individual.

"Riley!" Mesa pulls the young woman into a warm embrace. She is fancily dressed in a silk slip dress with tiny straps, a black leather jacket atop her shoulders, and black heels.

"Somebody looks a little too fancy for jail," Rivers teases as Mesa pulls away so Rivers can hug her.

"I AM too fancy for jail. I'm here for someone else," she chuckles nervously, and the two older men put on the same shocked expressions.

"Does little Riley have a date?" Rivers teases, causing her to turn red.

"Who is he? So, I can scare the idiot. He had better treat you nice or he's out of here," Mesa threatens seriously and Riley huffs.

"Yes, DAD. I'll be sure to tell you how it all goes when I return from the date," Riley scoffs before hitting his arm playfully.

"Want us to walk you?" Rivers offers but Riley puts her manicured hands out, a warning on her face.

"You will both remain here and not make a move! I'll leave now and go join my date. I just came to say hello, okay?" Riley warns and Mesa chuckles, amused by her antics.

"Enjoy your night, Riley. You deserve it." Riley makes a peace sign as she leaves the two men to their company.

"Are we drinking to this or what?" Rivers slaps his hands in excitement. Mesa eyes the pack of beers on the table.

"I think this calls for cognac, Rivers. Not that cheap thing you've got over there." Mesa chuckles.

Rivers' mouth falls open. "And where, for heaven's sake, will I find cognac?"

Mesa whistles as he heads for his desk and pulls out a huge bottle from his drawer. He taps it twice. "One of the finest you'll ever find. Chief Stuart gave it to me a while back and I drink it only on special occasions." Mesa pulls out two glasses, clinking them together. He pours cognac into the glasses and hands a glass to Rivers.

"I'll take a cigar afterward too," Rivers says as he takes a sip "This is good," he groans and Mesa nods, proud as he sips the cognac carefully. The two men fall into a comfortable silence as they sip their drinks.

"We've had a good run, Mesa. We really have," Rivers, muses as he faces Mesa, a nostalgic look in his eyes.

"Remember that case where we had to chase that mad woman? After she accidentally ate those cookies with---"

"With marijuana in them!" Mesa completes before bursting into a wild laugh. The two laugh loudly before clinking their glasses together.

"That was one crazy ride. I don't think I've ever seen a woman run that fast," Mesa snorts with laughter.

"Or that one time we chased the jewel thief through a cow farm?" Mesa bursts out laughing again, doubling over as the memory of it returns.

"THAT was epic!" Mesa cries as he holds his stomach. Rivers is busy hitting his thigh, tears slipping out as he cackles. When their laughter bubbles into deep breaths, Mesa exhales.

"That was arduous…"

Mesa's cellphone rings loudly, interrupting the conversation. Nodding apologetically at Rivers, Mesa picks the phone up.

"Detective Mesa speaking." There is no response, but Mesa can hear someone breathing heavily on the other end.

"Hello" Mesa says.

"I'm not sure what just happened but I've messed up," The voice is shaky and familiar. It takes Mesa a few seconds to place the voice and instantly, his brain goes into panic mode.

"I'm coming right away." Mesa says already understanding what has happened. Without another word, Mesa drops his glass of cognac on the table and rushes out of the office.

"Mesa, what's wrong?" Rivers yells but Mesa's mind is far-gone, barely hearing Rivers yell.

What has happened? Rivers asks again, getting no answer as Mesa runs out of the office.

Mesa's heart is thumping dangerously as he drives through the thick dark night.

When he told Emil, he could call him if he needed anything, he did not foresee this happening. Mesa, begins to mutter prayers under his breath for Emil. When he dashed out of the office, leaving Rivers behind, he realized he had no idea where he was going. When he called Emil again, the address he gave left his blood cold. There is only one reason Emil would go there and the thought scares Mesa more than anything.

His tires screech loudly as he parks his car in front of the apartment building. A couple of apartments are lit up and the building does not appear to have CCTV cameras. There is no one in the parking lot and no one at the entrance. Gently, Mesa steps out of the car. Pulling his gun out, he holds it in one hand as he closes the door of his car shut. Mesa moves in quickly to the inside of the building.

Quietly, Mesa moves towards the stairs, climbing two at a time, hoping that he runs into no one. The apartment is the second one on the second floor. Holding his gun firmly, Mesa opens the door gently. The door creaks softly as he makes his way inside and he is greeted with darkness.

"Emil?" Mesa calls out quietly as he closes the door behind him. A lamp comes on and Mesa sees him. Immediately, he tucks his gun back into his holster. Emil is seated by the lamp, his gaze on an adjacent wall, and there's a gun in his hand. Anxious, Mesa steps forward, holding his hand up but something stops him in his tracks. Emil's dark look.

"Emil." Emil does not respond. "Emil, what's wrong, son?" Mesa asks softly, taking another step forward. Emil is breathing hard and loud, his eyes glassy. Mesa follows his gaze and his breath hitches. No, Mesa says regretfully.

Propped against the wall with ropes around his body, bleeding profusely from bullet wounds is Nestor. Mesa holds back the cry that itches to break out of his throat. The blood has gathered into a small pool at Nestor's feet.

"Fuck!" Mesa whispers. "What the fuck happened? Oh, Emil, what did you do?" Mesa inches closer and places his hand underneath Nestor's nose. The man is clearly deceased, and his skin has begun to take on a blue shade. Mesa curses again and the old man begins to pace the room, his hands on his hips while Emil keeps staring at the bleeding body.

"I wasn't thinking. I just woke up and I came here with a gun," he reports quietly.

"What have you done?" Mesa mutters again, stopping to glance at the body. "Noooo, your family." Emil opens his mouth to speak but Mesa puts a handout.

"Don't say another word and wait for your attorney," He warns strictly but Emil shrugs a sad expression on his face.

"It's okay, detective," he says softly. When he looks at Mesa, his eyes are glassy with tears but there is no regret in them.

"He did not help my baby and because he neglected to be human, my baby was killed, so he needed to die," Emil explains in a soft voice, his gaze distant as he turns to stare at the body again. Mesa watches him with intense sorrow. Mesa's heart thuds loudly and he knows he will not leave the young man again, not this time around. The words he's about to say, lay heavily within his chest and he inhales deeply, feeling his moral compass dissolve and melt away.

"It was the final thing to do, detective. I'm so sorry I let you down," Emil adds.

Mesa interrupts, "Emil, go. I will take care of this, go to your family."

Emil's head turns toward him in shock. " Emil rises slowly, the gun still within his clutch as he shakes his head in refusal.

"No. I'm staying here. I did this and I will take care of it."

"Don't be stupid, Emil. You have a son and a wife who love you very much and need you. They have already lost too much; they can't lose you now" Mesa whispers gruffly. "Get your life back together, son. Mine is already about to end." Mesa inches closer and pulls the gun out of Emil's bloody hands. The tears roll out drop by drop as Emil stares at the old man.

"I can't let you do this. What is going to happen to your career? You have to---"

"YOU have to let me do this. It's the least I can do for everything," Mesa gives him a knowing look and Emil exhales, remembering.

"To be honest, Emil, after your court case, I stopped having a life. I owe you this. So, go," Mesa insists. The two men stay quiet as each man stands his ground, refusing to leave.

"I have nothing to lose, Emil. I have no one," Mesa whispers, placing a hand on his shoulder before pulling him into a tight hug. Emil chokes on a sob and squeezes the man just as tightly. Mesa feels the tension ease out of him as he keeps him in his arms and he relishes the moment. All this time, the guilt from Emil's case has haunted him and eaten deep into him, but now he can make amends. The young man sobs loudly in his arms and Mesa keeps him there until he regains composure. When he pulls back, his face red and stricken with tears, Emil gives him a shaky smile.

"I'll never forget this."

Mesa smiles in return. "Of course, you won't, but you have to promise me something. You won't ever make another mistake like this, stay with your wife and your son. If possible, make another baby." Emil smiles but Mesa grips his hand firmly to show his seriousness.

"Swear on Paola's life, Emil. Swear it now." The smile falls off Emil's face and he grips Mesa's hand just as firmly.

"I swear on Paola's life."

"Leave now. Run and never look back."

Horns blare as Emil runs along the road, barely hearing them. Sweat runs down his face and his chest is tight with every labored breath, but he pushes on, unable to bring himself to a stop. The image of Mesa kneeling in front of Nestor's body is etched in his mind and the words resonate in his head "Promise me you will never do this again."

The first time Emil really wanted to kill someone was when he was younger. After the court case with his stepdad, he really wanted to kill the judge. The man sentenced him to a life of abuse and violence. Emil wished he were an adult like his stepdad so he could show the judge what his stepdad was doing to him. The second time was when another man wanted to assault Sofia after his mom was also arrested. With his tiny fists and teeth, he tried his best to beat the man up, but one blow took him out. After that, Sofia was never the same and he swore never to let another person he loved go through such an ordeal. The third time was when Mesa told him about Ben and Nestor.

Nestor had not seen him coming. The idiot invited him into his house after he gave him the silly excuse of being one of the executives at from his job. The blow took him by surprise and before he could recover, Emil used the gun quickly. Right before his eyes, Nestor's face changed to Ben's, and he fired more shots than he had planned. Ben was there the day Paola went missing. He occasionally brought them meals and gave them advice. Once again, the person who brought him great sorrow and sadness was someone within his immediate environment. Emil makes a second promise to himself - Never again will he trust anyone aside from Caitlin and Junior. Never again will he let himself be comforted by a stranger.

Emil runs faster, hoping to outrun his demons and the fear pumping alongside the adrenaline. The distant sound of sirens reaches his ears, and they are quick to become faint. Mesa is going to prison for him. The realization nearly knocks him over, but he keeps running. When he sees the familiar markings of the new street his family now lives in, he presses on.

Their new house is nothing like their old one. With a lot of space around it and barely any bushes nearby, everything is within plain sight. Caitlin chose the house herself, traumatized by Paola's disappearance from their small house.

The scent of chicken wafts in the air as Emil runs unto the porch, sweaty and panting. He hurriedly opens the door with his key. When he closes it behind him, he takes in a deep breath, he quickly takes off his bloodied sweatshirt and cleans himself off with it. He slides down the door, burying his head in his hands. Tears threaten to pour out, but Emil holds them in, knowing Caitlin will be alarmed at the sight of tears and he needs to get cleaned up before she sees him. Finally, he got his revenge. Finally, it has come to an end.

Emil can hear Caitlin and junior laughing in the kitchen, talking noisily. He closes his eyes and listens to them, relishing the sound. While he roamed the streets, half-depressed and half-unstable, it was this sound that echoed in his dreams every day. It woke him up with a determination to do better and be better.

"Dad?" Emil's eyes pop open and he stares into his son's concerned brown eyes.

"Are you okay?" His son steps forward with a cautious look in his eyes. It is not until Emil gives him a megawatt smile that the anxiety eases out of Jr.'s eyes.

"I'm fine! I think I might have sprained something while running. I ran a little too hard," Emil chuckles as he puts a handout. "Help me up." Junior rushes towards him and with his help, Emil staggers up to his feet, smiling widely.

"You run a lot, Dad."

"I have to stay fit, son. Running is good for you, you know. Would help those little muscles of yours," Emil playfully tickles his arm, and junior inches away, chuckling.

"You always forget to take me along with you," Junior complains, folding his arms. Emil hisses through his teeth, "I'm so sorry. Tell you what? Tomorrow morning, let us go running together, okay? Is that fine?" Junior nods and his father ruffles his hair before making his way to the kitchen. Caitlin is leaning against a wall, a small smile on her face. At the sight of Caitlin, Emil finds his emotions welling up again, sinking to his knees with remorse and sorrow for Mesa's sacrifice.

Caitlin stares in shock, "Emil, what are you---"

He regains composure "I love you guys so much," Emil whispers as he hugs her legs tightly, his Adam's apple bobbing up and down. Caitlin chuckles nervously.

"Emil, you can tell me that with a hug, you know that?" She chuckles as she tries to pull him up, but he will not budge.

"Emil, come on, get up! Stop being silly!" Caitlin says softly. Emil pulls away slowly to stare into Caitlin's eyes. There are tears in her eyes as well.

"Get up and give me a hug, you big doofus," Caitlin sniffs. The two hold each other tightly. When Caitlin places her head on Emil's chest, Mesa's words ring heavily in his head again. Emil swears within himself not to break the promise.

"We should go on a date sometime. Just the two of us. I miss those days," Caitlin says quietly and her husband nods in agreement.

"Whenever you're ready, babe." Emil places a soft kiss on her lips.

"I really have to cook now, babe," Caitlin chuckles as the two pull apart with Emil smiling at her as she inches away.

"I'll be in the living room then." As Emil walks into the living room, he finds junior standing with arms akimbo in front of the television.

"In other news, Washington DC Police Detective was today arrested for the murder of one of his witnesses on a high-profile case...... Ben Smith VS the District of Columbia, a serial killer arrested a week ago," the reporter says and Emil's facial reaction changes.

"Change the channel, Junior. Let's focus on happy stories."

****

"I'm retiring," Rivers says.

Mesa's lips widen into a huge smile. "That's great, buddy! Congratulations!"

Rivers nods, his face glum. "Yeah. I figured since you are not going to be around anymore, I might as well leave now. Can't imagine working with anyone else."

Mesa nods as he fidgets slightly with the handcuffs around his hands. A tense silence fills the transport van. Ever since he was arrested, Rivers has been following him around, making sure to be the officer assigned to him. The news of his arrest shook the police force and while Mesa knows several officers are insistent on proving his innocence before a judge, he does not pay any attention to them.

"I'm guilty. Whatever punishment they want to give me, let them go ahead. I'm not afraid of anything," Mesa had told the chatty female lawyer Rivers got for him.

"Did you do it?" She had asked and all she got as a response was a blank stare.

"Do you want me to help you get those off?" Rivers asks kindly and Mesa shakes his head. They are a few minutes away from the facility. Though it feels strange to have the metal around his wrists, Mesa does not mind. He glances at his friend, whose forehead is scrunched in concentration, looking forward.

"I'll be fine, Rivers," Mesa says softly, drawing his attention. His friend's countenance softens lightly.

"You don't have to do this, Mesa. You know that right? You know that I don't believe you committed this crime."

Mesa sighs, leaning back against the truck, "Rivers---"

"No, Mesa. You haven't let me talk all through this trial. You refused to see me. You refused to talk to me about it. The few times I get to see you, and I bring it up, you shut me up. You and I both know that the last call you got before this whole thing was from Emil. You had no motive to kill this Nestor guy. If anything, he helped us."

Mesa sighs noisily. "So, what do you want from me, Rivers? What do you want me to say?"

"I want to know why you're doing this, Mesa. I want to know why you're throwing the rest of your life away for someone you barely know."

"So, you don't believe in goodness or kindness?" Mesa asks.

"People are motivated to do things for certain reasons. I want to know your reason," Rivers insists. Mesa falls quiet, staring at his legs.

"There's no reason, Rivers. How I see it is I get to save someone's life. I get to save someone's family from falling apart and that alone is enough for me."

Rivers shakes his head. "And finding his daughter's killer was not enough, Mesa? You had to lay down your own life and name? You're not Jesus Christ for fuck's sake."

Mesa shrugs. "It's a done deal already, Rivers. I just need you to be okay with it. Please."

"I'm not okay with it, Mesa. That's all I can say. You can do whatever you want but you can't tell me how to feel about it," Rivers looks away, his face grim. Mesa can feel the silent anger bubbling off him in waves.

"Will you at least come to visit?"

Rivers doesn't respond. Instead, he stares at Mesa, giving him a pointed look.

The former detective shrugs, "It was at least worth a shot."

The two stay quiet for the remainder of the ride. Mesa wonders what prison will be like. Though he knows it's going to be tough, he wonders if he will survive the rigors, given his age. Despite all his thoughts, the one thing that is absent is fear. Mesa is not afraid. When the truck stops moving, Mesa knows it is time. He meets his friend's concerned gaze with a small smile.

"Will you come to visit?" Mesa repeats quietly. Rivers put his hand out for a handshake. Mesa grabs it with both hands, letting him pull him in for a hug. The two friends stay in an embrace till someone hits the back of the truck loudly.

"I'll come every month. I've got no job to keep me occupied," Rivers' voice is sad as he pulls away.

Mesa nods, "I'm sorry, Rivers, I truly am."

"You're a fool but a good man. You'll be sorely missed out here in these parts."

The door is yanked open, and Mesa is roughly pulled out, his first introduction to the facility. It is the captain who welcomes him personally, taking him through the process. Mesa is quiet, obeying every instruction barked at him by the officers. He does not cower when they yell. He's hoping for the best – a quiet death within his cell. As long as he can have that, all will be well.

An officer is put in charge of taking Mesa to his cell and he follows meekly, remembering what it was like to be the one giving out instructions. The prison cells are small, they house two prisoners, two small bunks and a toilet.

"Off you go, Detective. Let me know if you need anything," The officer says quietly. Thanks Ogando, I really appreciate you, Mesa looks into his eyes, there's kindness there. The officer winks.

"We know you're not guilty," the officer whispers. Mesa walks inside the prison cell and there's a smug look on his face as he locks eyes with his cellmate. His cellmate jumps up and backward, his eyes wide in shock.

"No! Why are you here?" He cries, glancing behind him for help but there's none. The officer locks the cell and chuckling, he leaves the two cellmates.

"My retirement gift. I believe we will both have an amazing time together," Mesa chuckles as he inches closer to him. His cellmate inches backwards till his back is against the wall.

"I'm going to file a complaint immediately. You cannot be my cellmate."

"Says who? You?" Mesa cackles loudly like a deranged man. When his laughter dies, he glares at him.

"Now that I think about it, it's not your smile that gave you away, it's the lack of color on your face, however, I'll change that, I'm thinking a purple skin tone to your face will do your heart real good, and it's all free, a complement of your sister and those girls you smothered

And Ben, you're in for a terrible time."